MW01100606

Spire Publishing
www.spirepublishing.com

Muffin Heaven

by
Joe Hebden

Spire Publishing
www.spirepublishing.com

Spire Publishing, January 2008

Copyright © Joe Hebden

This book is sold subject to the condition that it shall not, by way of trade or otherwise, be lent, resold, hired out, or otherwise circulated without the publisher's prior consent in any form of binding or cover other than that in which it was published and without a similar condition including this condition being imposed on the subsequent publisher.

The moral right of Joe Hebden to be identified as the author of this work has been asserted.

First published in Canada 2008 by Spire Publishing.
Spire Publishing is a trademark of Adlibbed Ltd.

Note to Librarians: A cataloguing record for this book is available from the Library and Archives Canada. Visit www.collectionscanada.ca/amicus/index-e.html

Designed in Toronto, Canada
by Adlibbed Ltd.
Set in Baskerville and Baskerville Italics.
Printed and bound in the US or the UK
by Lightningsource Ltd.

ISBN: 1-897312-65-2

Spire Publishing

www.spirepublishing.com

1

I don't know why I'm sitting here trying to stop the flow of tears when there is nobody in this remote village to see, and today is the start of something new. I will dismiss what my grandmother often used to say: 'As one door closes, another shuts' and try to adopt the code outlined in The Guardian earlier this week.

It was merely an article about how one could learn to be happy, for those (like myself) who are not born to be naturally upbeat. My sceptical outlook would normally tend to dismiss such journalism, because if it doesn't come naturally then life must always be a struggle. This time I am tempted to give the techniques a try, such as noting down three things that went well today, which might be depressing if you can only think of one or two.

I've just had an email from my ex-boss, a very attractive lady in her early thirties, saying how much she values our *friendship*, which cleverly underlines that it is ridiculous for me to expect anything more – like enduring love and passion. She is keen to keep in touch; it has been entirely my decision to leave the office I've worked in for so long and attempt to open an establishment in the middle of nowhere called Muffin Heaven.

1.1

For me it will always come back to the home-made blueberry muffin, though these days there are so many outlandish varieties, like rhubarb and custard, honey and sesame or apple and prune. In the savoury arena there are some delights I can never tire of – Marmite (yeast extract) on toast, or eggs and bacon. A good blueberry muffin can be such a sweet and reliable companion, unless you have to watch the sugar intake, which will require a diabetic-friendly specimen.

It was my ex-boss Heather who inadvertently gave me the idea of opening some kind of eating establishment when she treated us all to the aforementioned rhubarb and custard muffin one chilly September afternoon. I watched her long, lean fingers break the fresh muffin into two large pieces, slowly stuffing those sweet lips with ever more sweetness.

'What do you think ?' she asked excitedly.

'Splendid !' I replied.

'Muffin heaven.'

At this comment from our lovely leader the whole office broke down in uncontrolled laughter, presumably because of some other meaning attached to the word muffin. Some more miserable colleagues looked at us in a disapproving manner, but they were only jealous of our special cakes, and of course Heather.

'Gorgeous' Kate chipped in.

'Mmmm' managed Rod between huge bites – he was supposed to be careful with eating and drinking, already taking tablets to boost poor thyroid activity.

'Is there any work going on over here ?' Peter asked

sarcastically, with that bloody grin that made me want to punch him very hard.

1.2

I'd forever had my eye on the ruined barn that commands such a fine position on the chalk brow above our small village. It's not so dramatic as the Himalayas or Alps, yet views over the Vale of York towards the western horizon never fail to lift flagging spirits.

There is no shortage of free water due to the thousands of springs that rise throughout the Yorkshire Wolds, and a modest wind turbine could generate most of our power. Such things are important considerations from both an environmental and economic point of view; I cannot envisage making much money from a lonely cafe that will appear as much part of the sky as land.

You might say that reproduction is the main purpose of life, but eating and drinking is rather important to sustain human existence, which will make Muffin Heaven much more than mere ornamentation.

'You'll have a load of old perverts banging on the door with a name like that' Rod had helpfully pointed out in my last week at the office.

'They'll soon realise that it's just food and drink on offer.'

'What about savoury muffins ?' suggested Eliza from the next group of desks.

'Never had one myself, perhaps we'll includes some cheese scones on the menu.'

Because of the wonderful view from the old barn I have started to investigate enormous windows on the Internet. The whole western wall must be toughened glass, allowing visitors to feel part of the sky, even a kind of Yorkshire heaven.

1.3

I have made no clear break with my past, indeed tonight is my leaving do (having already left) round the ancient and sometimes bloody streets of York on a Friday night. Heather has said she'll be there, and Kate, another dear colleague over many years, and several others – close and not so close workmates.

I will try not to show too much of the love that must already be so plain to ex-boss Heather, just concentrate on drinking plenty of ale and having a worry-free time.

When I actually departed a couple of days ago there was a small celebration at the Old White Swan over lunchtime when some senior staff literally showed their miserable faces for only five minutes. Others were more generous, as you'd expect after thirteen years in the same workspace.

Until Muffin Heaven is established there will be very few opportunities to meet with fellow humans, which is a major negative after so long in the same, busy working environment. I must not forget the important Guardian article on positive thinking, despite my inability to properly engage with any of the locals in this small, isolated village.

Our combined shop and post office has closed, leaving the Jolly Farmers pub and a thriving primary school as the only social hubs. There still remains a bus once or twice a week into the distant metropolis of York, where delightful Heather continues to labour in the old office with the extra burden of losing my occasionally helpful input.

1.4

Jonny One-Thumb has agreed to provide some DIY skills for converting the dilapidated stone barn into a thriving cafe and gathering point for lost souls, maybe even some ghosts as the site is right next to the Roman road into Malton.

He won't be able to start work immediately because of the unfortunate accident with a sharp knife that took off the top of his left thumb, exposing bone, and requiring urgent plastic surgery from a Greek lady doctor in Leeds.

I have always admired neon signs, and strongly believe that green neon will be ideal for our remote, rural location. Local planners will probably object, claiming it's not in keeping with the theme of Ryedale countryside, even though we are not within the Howardian Area of Outstanding Natural Beauty (AONB).

We were all surprised when a man so experienced in DIY sliced away the top of his thumb, but at the time he was being forced to perform an activity against his nature by a bisexual woman. It was in no way an obscure act of passion, merely a home maintenance job that didn't really need doing.

Jonny drove me up to the future site of Muffin Heaven last week, allowing us to properly assess costs, materials and labour. His driving was pretty good considering the large bandage on left thumb, though changing gear was proving slightly problematic.

'A fine view.'

'Do you think we'll get many customers ?' I asked.

'If the muffins are good' Jonny replied.

'I'm hoping to open next April or May.'

'That should be fine, if we don't get much snowfall.'

'No chance of that, with this global warming everyone's talking about.'

'I'll start in a few weeks then, at the end of November. If the doctor gives all clear.'

'Is she a beauty then, this Greek plastic surgeon ?'

'I can't deny there was some swelling in my trousers !'

1.5

It would be very difficult to achieve anything in this life without the help of others, and by happy accident I came across Kazia in York market a few weeks ago. She was serving on the hot food and drink stall near Little Shambles that provides an incredibly good value chip butty and other comfort food.

There are so many Poles in this country at the moment, most doing jobs that long-time residents of the UK wouldn't touch with a bargepole. Others are in better-paid employment such as dentistry – six out of eight dentists at my National Health Service practice are Polish !

Kazia is a cheerful, friendly lass in her twenties, with thick, blonde hair tied firmly back and bright blue eyes shining from an attractive, slim face. She tells me about working on the market, and I tell her about my plans for Muffin Heaven.

'I have car, not very good, but I could work for you – Yes ?!'

'Don't you like working here ?'

'It OK, but the boss has the wandering hands.'

'Do you have a mobile number ? I'll ring you after Christmas, when we've made some progress with the building.'

Kazia gave a lovely warm smile, and I knew I could trust her, partly because she needed a decent job and partly because of the gut feelings about people I've developed to a fine art over the years.

She didn't charge me for the butty, or the strong Yorkshire tea you could almost stand a teaspoon up in. I wandered into King's Square adjacent to the market, trying to find a quiet spot for stuffing my face away from irritating pigeons. Things were very slowly starting to take shape in reality and in my mind regarding Muffin Heaven; I sat in the welcome autumn sunshine, enjoying a splendid chip butty and occasionally sipping tea.

1.6

This is a difficult time between the certainty of being a wage slave and the establishment of something new. I wish that my former boss Heather would drive to our lonely village, just to give a powerful hug and reassure me everything will be alright. Most of the time I am now spending alone, which feels very strange after many years of enforced socialising in the office; I may need to buy the book on positive thinking as it will be all too easy to allow negative feelings to envelop me.

The opening of Muffin Heaven seems a long way off, with many practical problems to overcome; I must focus on the many opportunities a cafe will offer for human interaction and a new way of living.

In our village I have no friends, only people that might say hello; it is not like the town where you can easily go shopping, to a pub or cafe, the cinema or whatever takes your fancy. We have a good pub, which only opens in the evening, but this is not much use as we can't take our young children with us.

All being well these are only temporary problems, because Muffin Heaven will provide an excellent focus for our scattered rural population, including educational and exercise opportunities, such as T'ai Chi on Tuesday and romantic poetry on Thursday.

I still need Heather now. I dreamt about her last night. We were preparing for my leaving do, but instead of the focus being on the party it was the imminent appearance of some handsome bloke that Heather had fancied for months. A dream to shatter all my silly fantasies of intimacy with a physically inspiring woman.

1.7

The first thing to do with the old barn is to make it weather tight by repairing what's left of the red-tiled roof. The farmer has virtually given the structure away with my promise of free food and drink for himself and family for as long as Muffin Heaven prospers.

I am greatly helped by the modest voluntary redundancy payment from my Civil Service benefactors who are fulfilling the Labour Government's vote-winning strategy of 'losing' thousands of experienced staff. For some reason the great British public feel there is no place for people contributing to important areas of our lives, such as environment, food and rural affairs (in my own case).

I've had a message from ex-colleague Eliza this morning - I would choose to marry her above anyone else because of her excellent sense of humour and DD bust. This is unlikely to happen because of my own partner and children, and despite the fact Eliza has recently left a long-term lesbian relationship I'm sure she'd be looking for somebody much younger, sporty and probably female.

A few weeks ago, before my leaving, another lesbian lass was departing our office, which meant the usual visit to the Old White Swan for a few drinks. Eliza had been at home that morning and had clearly spent a few hours making herself look pretty, because she looked really stunning as she came into the bar. If I get the chance I must remember to tell her that, because it's true, and I would very much like to see her smile wickedly again.

Through the farmer that sold me the barn and adjacent land

I've got a good deal on restoring the roof, as his son's in the building trade. It will be a struggle to 'seal' the building before the real winter sets in; it feels bloody cold today for the beginning of November, despite cloudless blue skies over our small Wolds village.

A lingering kiss from Heather, Eliza or Kate is all I need to truly warm my lonely soul..........is it too much to ask ?

1.8

Heather has been kind enough to send through a 'best ever' blueberry muffin recipe to take its place on the new menu. Occasionally, she would bring her cakes to the office, and they were always deliciously moist (like herself). The main reason for their success was sticking rigidly and carefully to the finest recipes, which is exactly what you'd expect any self-respecting Virgo lady to do. This is totally the opposite of my own approach, relying on so-called intuition and inspiration, which is why it would be really useful to have Heather on the team for the new venture.

Heather's Best Ever Blueberry Muffins

Preparation time overnight
Cooking time 10 to 30 mins

Ingredients

110g/4oz plain flour
110g/4oz butter
65g/2½oz caster sugar
2 eggs
1½ tsp baking powder
125g/4½oz blueberries, or equivalent in frozen blueberries
pinch nutmeg

Method

1. Cream the butter and sugar together then slowly add the eggs, mix for 3 minutes. Add the flour, baking powder, nutmeg, and refrigerate for at least an hour, preferably overnight.
2. Place a spoonful of muffin mixture into each muffin case, filling each to just over half way. Stud each muffin with about 8 blueberries.
3. Bake in an oven set at 200C/400F/Gas 6 for 20 minutes or until golden on top.

Sounds simple enough..............with some practice............

1.9

Because I have no religion - which is very fortunate considering the extreme actions of one Jehovah's Witness in the news who died after giving birth to twins, because no blood transfusion was permitted - I frequently refer to the I Ching as a source of ancient wisdom.

Modesty is a highly prized virtue in the text that I always try to emulate in a genuine open-hearted manner, rather than some artificial display of under-selling oneself. I haven't dared to seek guidance about Muffin Heaven, preferring to learn from direct experience if this is the right way for me.

I have often sought answers to questions regarding Heather when common sense tells me that we can never be together in any meaningful way. Yet my feelings for her are so powerful that I always return to her beauty (sometimes accompanied by her loud swearing).

It was true that among close colleagues in the office swearing would often play a part in our daily banter, and sometimes cause offence to some stuffy co-workers. But it did serve to strengthen our bonds in the face of nonsensical management decisions and the often mind-numbing boredom of our work.

The contrast between Heather's heavenly features and the less than heavenly language that often spilled from her lips could be shocking to the uninitiated, but to the in-crowd it was a robust delight.

It will be very painful if I do lose touch with Heather, Kate and others, but it seemed long overdue that I had to find something more meaningful than the Civil Service. For me Muffin Heaven will not be just a cafe, but also a scheme to boost the level of happiness in a sometimes empty rural environment. If we can't get the Dalai Lama to open our venue (down with China, Free Tibet !) it will have to be President of the UK Muffin Club.

2

The phone rang, but all I could hear on the other end was a woman crying.

'Who is it ?'

More crying.

'Hello ?'

'It's Kazia.'

'What's happened ?'

'That bastard, he feel my tits !'

'You mean your boss ?'

More tears.

'Do you want to come over for a chat ?'

'Is that OK..........your wife ?'

'We're not married; and she knows all about you anyway.'

'I will drive.'

'Take the road to Stamford Bridge and turn off towards Buttercrambe.'

Kazia finally arrived at eight o' clock on a very dark evening, and the two kids rushed to let her in.

'Don't scare her' I shouted.

She looked just as attractive as I'd remembered with a great big smile directed at the children.

'Come in, I'll get you a brandy.'

'Do you have vodka ?'

I guided her away from the lounge where the kids had been watching telly into our small dining room. After a brief introduction to Mary (my partner) we settled down with large glasses of clear, throat-burning liquid.

'I can't go on working there.'

'Muffin Heaven won't be open for ages yet. Is there anywhere else you can go ?'

'Not really.' Kazia burst into tears.

'I'll talk to Mary, you might be able to help with the kids, and some preparations for opening our cafe.'

Kazia's tear-stained face brightened, and it seemed we'd found a house guest for the next several months.

2.1

To try and maintain a link with my ex-colleagues I have arranged a gift pack of 12 assorted muffins to be delivered to their office with a sexually suggestive card. I am fairly sure it will not cause offence as sexual innuendo was a large part of the daily banter that enlivened our dreary lives. It would have been good practice to bake the muffins myself, however a simple search of the Internet gave a range of companies specialising in baked items by courier.

I am still awaiting the magic email from Heather saying that she's finally realised I love her and she's got a growing fondness for me. This remains highly unlikely for many reasons, including a very thick address book of all her friends, indicating a lively and fulfilling social life. This couldn't be much more different from my lonely self, though we do now have Kazia spending much of her time with the family.

I took a walk up onto the high Wold this morning to see how far the farmer's lad had got on with the roof, and it looked quite promising with a blue plastic underlay awaiting all the neatly stacked tiles below. The wind was fairly strong, but the usual amazing view was on offer as I easily picked-out York Minster and other local landmarks.

I am more concerned about the massive west window that is going to be so expensive, even if imported from the Czech Republic. It would be very disappointing to bung in some ordinary BOGOF (buy one get one free) white plastic framed household windows, but I'm not keen on begging in front of any bank managers for extra funds.

Heather would be fantastic at putting together a business

case for these financial folk, but for me they are not even speaking the same language. She continues to labour in a job she no longer enjoys, and seems unable to take any decisive action about doing something different. The level of swearing can only increase until one day a senior manager will ask her to clear that messy desk for the last time.

2.2

It feels strange to have Kazia living in the garage like a dangerous dog, though we have done our best to make everything comfortable with winter coming on. She seems happy enough, sharing all our meals, playing with the children, trying out muffin recipes and obscure Polish dishes.

I wonder if she'll make a good partner for Jonny One-Thumb who has always failed to find a suitable woman, and often seems to go out of his way to date unsuitable ladies. At least he has the DIY to keep busy – his left thumb is almost healed and ready to get stuck-in to Muffin Heaven's interior.

I must put it down to my new positive thinking approach, because we've had some luck on the large expanse of glass needed to fully appreciate the remarkable view. I sent loads of enquiries from websites and ninety percent didn't even respond, but a small firm from Selby (only twenty miles away) are very excited about the project and will be providing a detailed quote soon.

I've been up on the Wold again this morning taking photographs with a new digital camera as I'm keen to get a simple website available quickly to commence the whetting of local appetites.

The wind was cold up there, which made me think about the need for a couple of log burning stoves – even some summer days can be rather chilly in such an exposed position. The area is quite popular with ramblers and cyclists, and I know they will like nothing more than a real fire to warm nithered fingers and toes.

There used to be a Youth Hostel in the nearby village of

Thixendale, but the car has destroyed so much, including many of these resting places no longer deemed necessary. It still remains a remarkable road down the steep-sided chalk valley to Thixendale from Leavening Brow – only ragged sheep for company all those meandering, green miles.

2.3

Eventually, I'll get used to this loneliness, with Mary at work, kids at school and Kazia visiting Polish pals in York. At least I have an insane cat for company – always chasing something or knocking something else off the windowsill.

Things will pick-up soon when Jonny can start work on the cafe interior, which will be all bare stone and wooden floors. I saw an interesting TV programme recently where a couple were restoring a so-called 'bastle' in Northumberland – a cross between a barn and a castle – useful for defending oneself against hostile forces many years ago in the borderlands.

We don't have any genuine marauders in the Yorkshire Wolds these days, but I do see Muffin Heaven as a safe retreat – both physical and spiritual, though most people will be only interested in stuffing themselves. Simplicity must be the guiding principle, for the building, for the catering, and the way we communicate with 'customers' in a direct and friendly Yorkshire manner.

There is no visible sign of human life in our village this morning; only fifteen miles from the buzzing city of York, but it might as well be many miles further. Thick grey clouds are moving swiftly eastwards, though we are promised a sunnier and slightly warmer afternoon.

It's a while since I've ridden my motorbike round the narrow country lanes, but I can pick and choose a nice warm day to go out now I've left the office – it is November, when the tendency is to more freezing weather.

The telephone sounds its brutal interruption to my thoughts.

'Is that roof done yet ?'
'Just another week or so Jonny.'
'I'm keen to get started now the thumb's better.'
'I don't think you've met Kazia yet, have you ?'

2.4

The afternoon sky has cleared to brilliant blue as promised, though some gusts of wind are rattling the door and window frames. I feel more human after a nice lunch washed down with lashings of strong tea.

'Hello.'

'Is that you Kazia ?'

'Yes, I been to the Pole shop in Walmgate.'

The poor lass is laden with shopping bags, which she drops on the kitchen table in front of me.

'Have you ever tried our cherry vodka ?'

'Not in the afternoon, or evening come to that.'

She grabs two tall, slim glasses from the cupboard and pours a silly amount into each.

'This will make us forget the wind !'

Vodka on its own can be rather challenging, but accompanied by a subtle cherry flavour is most agreeable on a late autumn afternoon.

'Thank you for letting me stay.'

'That's OK, you'll be helping us at Muffin Heaven next spring.'

The sudden injection of alcohol made me notice Kazia's lovely features more intensely, and I wished to be a free agent, and a few years younger. She poured more cherry vodka, and the chill that had been in my legs and heart melted away like the late frost of May.

2.5

Now I've given up official full-time employment it's possible to consider getting a dog for the first time, which I know will delight the kids and Mary. I hope Kazia is a dog lover, because it'll probably have to share the garage with her.

I've been looking through the book Observers Dogs, and my favourite so far is the TT (Tibetan Terrier), which they describe as 'not unlike an Old English Sheepdog in miniature'. What appeals to me is the Tibetan connection, a culture that has always fascinated, and raised my blood pressure due to the appalling acts of Chinese Government forces regarding this peaceful nation.

It might prove to be the ideal companion for the vaguely spiritual venture of Muffin Heaven, which will be perched like a tiny monastery on the edge of these Yorkshire Wolds. I'm not sure what the hygiene regulations are regarding the owner's dog trotting around your own cafe, but we can always allow the TT to run about outside in comfort due to a double coat of long fur.

My daughter has prepared a long list of small or medium dogs, and I know Mary would like a Maltese as this was the toy beast fondly remembered from childhood in remote Lincolnshire. There are so many factors to consider, like cost of purchase, cost of feeding, cost of kennels if you go away, vet bills, having to walk them all the time (and clear up the shit).

Kate, who I've left behind in the Civil Service office, would never stop talking about her soppy Field Spaniel, who is very much a child in dog form, treated to all kinds of actual and emotional luxuries. I would never want to establish an unhealthily close relationship with a canine, but as my Gran would often repeat: 'the more I see of men, the more I like dogs.' She was so fond of these sayings, dear old Gran, usually so very acidic.

The most likely outcome is that a local farmer will offer us a cute puppy, of a breed we haven't considered, and Mary and the kids will be hooked. So much for dreams of a Tibetan outpost in Yorkshire..........

2.6

I have been battling the black dog of depression these last few days, not that I've a great deal to complain about except feelings of isolation and uncertainty about the future. The book I ordered on positive thinking has not yet arrived; more importantly I have had no communications from my supposedly close ex-colleagues Kate and Heather.

I remain fairly certain that I will not slip into the hideous mental state of late teenage years, when I ended up having electric shock treatment. Many so-called mental hospitals have closed now anyway, which means you've got to get your electric shocks and other treatment in the 'community'.

If only we had genuinely close-knit communities, like the remote Amazonian tribes, where such things as homes for old people don't exist, where problems remain part of the entire group and not isolated from it. I am no doubt slipping into a romanticised view of tribal people, but 'advanced' countries like the UK have lost so many simple values.

It's spectacularly blue today, though fucking cold, and I can't afford to have heating on during daylight hours. This will change when we have our wood burning stoves at Muffin Heaven, but for now it must be a quick session on the exercise bike and a warm, fleecy jacket.

It would be better not to care whether anyone sends me a jolly email, but I do, as I've never been one of these thick-skinned types or possessing the magical properties of a duck's back in relation to water.

My toes are cold, yet I'm determined to remain positive; the new roof is almost finished, and Kazia has another bottle of cherry vodka stashed – when she returns from a long walk round Burythorpe.

2.7

Jonny One-Thumb was kind enough to take us to a place that I've always regarded as a natural wonder, but have not visited for many years. The Hebden Bridge and Heptonstall area in the West Yorkshire Pennines is much more dramatic than my own Yorkshire Wolds, and very different in terms of its industrial heritage.

In some ways it is sad that Hebden Bridge has become mainly a tourist and commuter town, losing the powerful local identity that developed from packhorse days through to textile mills. It is surely good that the worst exploitation has disappeared with these factories, along with their detrimental impact on health and general well-being.

The picturesque town is now a delight for the lover of gift shops and anybody (like myself) intending to open a cafe. There are so many examples of places to eat and drink that it would be very hard not to learn which are doing it right. We went to a friendly place next to the babbling and burbling Hebden itself, and close to the weathered stone bridge that gives the place its name.

In recent months there has been little rain in Yorkshire and so many bright, sunny days, however I was not particularly surprised that the Calder Valley was grey, damp and very windy. Jonny expressed some disbelief as we travelled from Halifax through a village called Friendly, which neither of us could remember from previous visits. The residents must have campaigned to proudly label their little community with a warm and welcoming tag, contrasting with the often bitter weather.

The waterside cafe offered a wide menu of simple dishes and an extensive range of cakes and puddings. The Welsh rarebit I had was more the consistency of scrambled egg rather than the usually firmer cheesy example, but nonetheless very tasty.

'Lots of lesbians round here' Jonny commented.

'Keep your voice down.'

'Vegans, lesbians, co-operatives, political correctness.'

'The clientele seem fairly ordinary here.'

'Don't be fooled.'

'We can't have this sort of talk at Muffin Heaven.'

'Don't worry, I'm only doing the DIY.'

The grey sky appeared to be brightening with a small patch of blue over the Rochdale Canal, and we drove the steep road to little Heptonstall village perched high above Hebden Bridge. I forced poor Jonny to help me find the grave of American poet Sylvia Plath in the bleak, windswept churchyard, and eventually we located the simple burial with a few bright offerings from her followers. It still feels strange that someone who had no real sympathy or liking for the area, and who probably belongs back in the United States should be laid to rest in such a lonely spot so far from home. It seems even more peculiar when her husband Ted Hughes, the poet who was born nearby, is buried elsewhere in England.

2.8

A return to more settled sunny weather allowed the finishing touches to be put to the red-tiled roof of the old stone barn. There was a strong feeling of security provided by sealing the top of the building, which was now mostly weather tight as the window sockets were blocked with temporary clear plastic sheeting. It would be a few weeks before the custom-made windows were ready, but there was nothing to stop development of the interior as far as walls and flooring were concerned.

A heavy oak door was being made at the nearby timber yard on the Birdsall estate, which would last many decades of even the worst Wolds weather, and abuse by all those entering and leaving our remote cafe. Some proper bicycle stands would be needed, and a solid boot-scraper to remove the worst of muck attached to walking boots. I am already firmly committed to charging less for those arriving on foot or pedal cycle, as this is both an environmentally and aesthetically sound policy to discourage excessive car use.

Birdsall estate had delivered the carefully measured joists and floorboards, which were waiting the creative input of Jonny One-Thumb.

'I'll be up there tomorrow, whatever the weather.'

'It won't matter as we'll be under cover – the finished roof looks grand.'

'I'll bring a gas stove so we can have a frequent brew, and get some bacon and eggs spitting in the pan.'

'The remainder of your thumb is OK then ?'

'That's what the Greek lady said !'

With the roofing team gone, and before Jonny arrived, was a special time up at Muffin Heaven. Just to sit there with a flask of strong tea and some biscuits made by Kazia, gazing into the dreamy distance beyond the Vale of York, full of hope for whatever the future might bring.

It appears that I might well have upset my former office colleagues in some way, because there is still no word from Heather, Kate or even Eliza. I have seemingly already become an outcast from the peculiar world of Civil Service administration that remains so wanting of a sense of humour.

2.9

Thanks to the Internet it is all too easy to access material on any subject from pornography to muffins, and of course both together. I have just come across the site muffinrecipes. co.uk that is strictly focused on baking only, featuring new recipes for strawberry and cream muffins, chocolate muffins with white chocolate chips and delightful lemon muffins.

The many sections listed include: how to make muffins, classic muffins, muffins with fruit or berries, muffins with chocolate, seasonal muffins, savoury muffins and muffin book reviews.

'What do you think of these recipes Kazia ?'

'Very nice, but I will be able to do the Polish dishes ?'

'What do you have in mind ?'

'Bigos.'

'Lovely, what exactly is it ?'

'Hunter's stew, with sausage, smoked pork, sauerkraut and many other things.'

'Perfect for the Yorkshire Wolds, where we still see plenty of shooting.'

'People will want the meals and the muffins, yes ?'

'You're absolutely right Kazia, we must cater for savoury and sweet.'

'I will make you Bigos, you will see.'

She is much more relaxed and naturally cheerful since coming to stay in our garage, and her young, clear eyes shine like the brightest full moon over the Tatra mountains. Kazia was particularly pleased when the wood-burning stoves arrived that will provide heating in Muffin Heaven, but for the next few months of winter will make her temporary home so cosy.

We spent an enjoyable morning clearing out one corner of the garage for storing a full load of seasoned timber; physical work can be so much more satisfying than the many years I spent sitting on my arse in that dreadful office.

3

The positive thinking book I ordered last week has still not arrived ! Surely they should ensure next day delivery for this type of subject matter because they don't know just how desperate the potential recipient is. I am managing to remain reasonably upbeat despite the lack of social interaction beyond immediate family and Kazia (who is often at the Polish social club in York).

When we get nearer the opening of Muffin Heaven it will be necessary to explore further staffing options, as one young Polish woman will not be enough. I'm keen to give those who really need a break priority, because I've often experienced the nonsense of interviews, not having the right qualifications, or the right suit and tie. It is more important to find somebody trustworthy and with a good heart, rather than all the other crap.

I've just heard from an ex-colleague that he'll be taking voluntary redundancy as well next spring, though I don't think he'd be suited to our new venture. If things go on as they are fewer and fewer Civil Servants will be available to process the same amount of work, leading to personal and Governmental meltdown.

Jonny One-Thumb is managing fine with his remaining fingers, and has most of the wooden floor lain already. I can't decide if it will be best to have it highly varnished to aid cleaning, or leave it completely untreated, allowing the development of its own character over the years.

'It's already been sprayed to prevent rot, so no need to do anything else.'

'You're probably right Jonny, but these hygiene inspectors might find fault with roughly finished wood.'

'Hardly roughly finished.'

'I'm always inclined to the natural way, so we'll no doubt just leave it.'

'When are the windows coming ?'

'A few more days. We'll need a crane to get the big one in.'

'Don't worry, it'll be fine.'

I am excited and nervous about our giant west window that should provide an almost 180 degree view of North Yorkshire countryside. In summer visitors will also be able sit in the open air, allowing further communion with the great outdoors.

3.1

The dream girls of my former life may or may not have severed their ties with me forever, but I will never forget the heavenly form of Heather in particular. She has inspired me, like the landscape around Hebden Bridge, over so many years, that it is now impossible to separate my love for her from my own self.

I have publicly been too honest in my opinions about some of my ex-colleagues, but their hypocrisy is extraordinary as they've said similar things many times behind closed doors of the tea room or ladies toilet.

It would have been good to spend at least one night with Heather, if only to find that she was less than I'd imagined, but surely the reality of experiencing her lovely body against mine would be so much better than the bleak hours of many empty days.

Brief hugs are all I have known, not even a lingering kiss that would reveal the true nature of our souls to each other. I am not content with fleeting glances into her dark brown eyes, and the occasional accidental brush against that pale skin.

Though it is less than two weeks since we last met I'm already wondering if that was the last I'll see of her, with all that unnecessary make-up and the fancy clothes that other girls must appreciate more than men. Now I don't even have a photograph – I could have kept images of her, but they seem so pale in comparison to the real thing.

Men are supposed to be uncaring, moving swiftly to the next shag, and many might be like that, and must be in purely reproductive terms, yet for me there will always be tenderness and the hope of something deeper and truly meaningful.

3.2

Emma invited our young lad to play with her kids on the way home from the village school for the final forty-five minutes of precious daylight that remained on a bright November afternoon. She is friendlier than many of the mums who are more concerned about their place on the social ladder; Emma is also the daughter of a lady who helps at the school as a teaching assistant for slower students.

'I see you're rebuilding the old barn.'

'We're opening a cafe – Muffin Heaven.'

Emma giggled.

'Any jobs going ?'

'We're opening in spring, if you're genuinely interested.'

'I need the money, for the two girls.'

Our young lad was happy to be left with other children, rather than return to his own boring home to watch TV. In the summer he would play outside until late, but these winter nights are very restrictive for energetic kids.

'Just pop back in an hour to pick him up.'

'Thanks for letting him play.'

My impression of her was a natural, no-nonsense person who would fit in well with Kazia and the enterprise as a whole. It remained to be seen if our casual conversation would amount to anything when Muffin Heaven was due for its grand opening.

I'd had a call about fitting the small wind turbine that would provide our modest electrical needs; cooking would have to be mostly from giant gas bottles, unless the wind was particularly strong. Because of our remote position there was no objection from local planners about noise or spoiling the natural beauty of the Yorkshire Wolds with a small windmill.

Chatting briefly with Emma had shown there were some limited social opportunities in the village, which would of course be greatly boosted by our own unique outlet for body and soul.

3.3

There are very few streams in the chalk valleys of our Yorkshire Wolds, however we are lucky to have countless springs bubbling up all over the place. When I purchased the old barn it came with a choice of two springs that might be suitable for Muffin Heaven's water supply.

In these days of strict regulation I had to pay Yorkshire Water to test the spring quality and install a pipe to the barn. I have fortunately escaped the provision of a water meter and charging for my own water, but they will be billing me for an annual inspection to ensure a healthy and safe supply to the public.

I'm sure that using pure Wolds water rather than the chemically enhanced mains supply will appeal to many of our visitors; we are very fortunate to live in a part of the world that rarely suffers drought, though this might be subject to the vagaries of climate change.

When up at the barn to see how Jonny was progressing it occurred to me that the nearest library is many miles away, and with the popularity of free book exchanges we can devote one large wall to bookshelves.

I have often used the Bookcrossing website, which allows you to rate books that are then left in a public place for others to pick-up, read, and pass on. In theory a popular title could travel many times around the world until it finally disintegrates or finds a true home.

'What do you think about making the entire north wall into shelving ?'

'Big job. I've got to seal all the cracks with mortar first, and it won't be easy getting true horizontals in a higgledy-piggledy place like this.'

'You're not a big reader, are you Jonny ?'

'I don't mind travel guides or books of photographs.'

'I'm sure we can manage some of those in the collection. I'll speak to Birdsall again about the wood.'

Jonny was getting used to these sudden new ideas that always meant extra work for himself, though he was enjoying the rural peace, and wondered if there might be any long-term role at Muffin Heaven.

3.4

The sound of a giant crane struggling up the steep hill out of our village could only mean one thing – the windows had arrived ! The glass was already at the old barn as we watched the lorry and crane battle the tough gradient. Unless the vehicle could make it up, there would be no chance of lifting the west window into place, let alone the smaller ones.

The team from Selby who had made and would fit them watched the slow progress calmly and quietly, along with several interested locals who hadn't seen anything so exciting since the wartime bomber had crashed on Leavening Brow in the 1940s.

'What do you reckon Jonny ?'

'They should have come Garrowby way, instead of through Leavening.'

'Is the lorry gonna get round the corner there ?'

'Might just do it.'

Emma had walked up with her two kids, who were blissfully unconcerned about the whole operation.

'Shouldn't be long now' she said positively.

'They might have to turn round.'

Eventually, with plenty of tight manoeuvres the lorry and crane was positioned next to Muffin Heaven, and four smaller windows were lifted in on the east and south side, then secured by the Selby lads. All went very quiet as the massive final window was lifted into the air above the red-tiled roof and suspended for what felt like an eternity.

'I can't look !'

'Don't panic' Jonny said calmly.

'We can't afford to replace it if they drop it.'

To walk through the heavy oak door and see the great west window slotting perfectly into place was very moving, particularly as the view revealed after so long behind plastic was truly awe-inspiring.

3.5

I'd encouraged Kazia and Jonny to meet for a Friday night session at the Little Angel, our friendly local pub. Kazia was pretty enthusiastic from the off, but Jonny was showing the usual reticence that meant he was still living alone in a messy house full of tools and gadgets. Most men would jump at the chance of a date with someone like Kazia, but Jonny One-Thumb is a strange character bred from strange parents.

The Little Angel can be fairly raucous at weekends, though we've hardly visited since the kids were born, slipping into the easy routine of telly and early nights. We would regularly go to the Theatre Royal in York or see a band on the verge of making it big at Fibbers – now it's just Coronation Street or Wife Swap.

Jonny arrived at the pub first around 8.30, ordering just a half of lager to steady his nerves. There was only one small table left, because the place had already been taken over by a half-pissed assortment of farm labourers and stable lads. In my experience it is often the tiny jockeys who are most aggressive, feeling they have to prove themselves 'taller' than they are.

'Hello.' Kazia surprised Jonny by coming in the side door.

'Hello. What would you like to drink ?'

'I try lager, same as you.'

After fifteen minutes fighting his way to the bar Jonny finally returned with two pints.

'Sorry, it's rather busy tonight.'

'No problem.'

They sat in silence for a few moments as Jonny noticed just

how attractive his companion was.

'Is Muffin Heaven finished yet ?' Kazia asked.

'It'll be a while yet. I hear you were working on the market ?'

Kazia went quiet and her eyes filled-up with tears.

'I'm sorry, I didn't mean to upset you.'

She then told him the whole sorry tale, of coming to England to earn money for her family in Poland, and how the stall owner had tried to fondle her.

'I need a strong drink.'

Jonny battled his way to the bar again, shell-shocked by Kazia's account of crude exploitation.

'I've got us both double Jack Daniels with diet Coke.'

'I never try this before.'

'You'll be looking forward to our cafe opening then ?'

'Of course, your friend is very kind.'

Kazia returned to her natural smiley state, and Jonny found himself gazing into her remarkable blue eyes.

3.6

I decided to blow the cobwebs away with a late morning ride on my Benelli Velvet 250 all the way along the chalk escarpment to the neat market town of Pocklington. It was a brilliant, blue day, and despite a temperature of only seven Celsius all was very comfortable in a selection of warm clothing. It felt like a kind of proof that I could actually escape the village for a while, even though winter was fast approaching - I can't drive a car, and buses are rarer than a straight man in the clergy.

I only bought a few essentials at the small supermarket – bread, red wine, sensitive toothpaste, whisky, and a copy of Heat magazine for the horoscope and other nonsense. The shop was full of old people (is Thursday when they're paid some pension ?), which proved quite annoying for somebody always in a hurry.

The Wolds looked spectacular in blinding sunshine, though the Vale of York itself was still a little misty. The major hazard apart from excessive brightness were the usual dumb pheasants that are incapable of running the correct way off narrow roads. Givendale village was lovely as ever in vivid autumn leaf colour, with the little stone church, a series of adjoining ponds, and gentle hills crowding together as background.

It is still only two weeks since I left the office, and I find myself wishing that Heather would send me a message to say all is OK, any transgressions are forgiven, but nothing except bloody spam in my email inbox. I keep telling myself to remain positive and look to the future, yet I crave the approval of this beautiful woman, now more than ever.

The blue sky towards York is very much a lonely sky; perhaps Heather and Kate haven't taken offence, but are too busy in the office, or simply can't be bothered to get in touch. It seems increasingly unlikely that I'll get an invite to the office Christmas lunch or any festive piss-up round town, which is a relief in some ways because of those ex-colleagues I would rather not meet.

I will try to focus on the development of Muffin Heaven – the many details that must be worked on before our glorious opening next year.

3.7

'I'm running a bit short of cash for cookers, kitchen equipment, tables, chairs – might have to grovel to the bank after all.'

'Actually, I've been thinking of getting more involved' Jonny replied.

Both were standing in the church-like empty interior of Muffin Heaven, structurally complete and sealed against Yorkshire weather.

'I've got some money that my mum left me, and nothing else lined-up after fitting-out this place.'

'It'll be quite some time till you see any financial return, if ever.'

'Maybe, but I believe it's a good project.'

'How did you and Kazia get on the other night ?'

'Not bad, she's taking me to the Polish social club in Bradford on Saturday.'

'Is that near where the policewoman was shot ?'

'Yes, but she says the Polish folk are more friendly.'

A friendship since 1982 meant there was no doubt that Jonny would honour the promise of providing extra funds, and all being well the purchase of a dedicated muffin oven.

'I'll get to work on the wiring then.'

'Good. I've got to ring a Chinese fella in Malton about teaching some T'ai Chi classes.'

3.8

We had often visited the Chinese take away near the library in Malton without realising that the little old chap in the corner was a keen practitioner of T'ai Chi. I suppose we'd always been more concerned about ordering the crispy duck, spare ribs or chicken chop suey - hardly knowing what the ancient Oriental movements were.

'You are here for my father' said the middle-aged lady behind the counter.

'Yes, thank you.'

'Do you know how old he is ?'

'No idea.'

'Eighty-three next April.'

'Amazing. Do you think he'll be OK taking classes ?'

The lady just laughed, and continued packing boxes of food into a white plastic bag.

I sat nervously by the window, realising that this was another example of a catering outlet that might be able to give us some pointers. There was no reason why we couldn't serve some simple rice or noodle dishes; the muffins would always be there for those tempted by sweetness.

'Hello.'

The old man bowed, looking much more like a person of around sixty; without speaking he began a series of gentle, coordinated and rhythmic movements that amazed me and the few customers waiting for pork balls or Chinese chips with gravy.

'Can you come once a fortnight from next April ?'

'April my birthday. Yes.'

'We're opening a cafe called Muffin Heaven, and....'
I was interrupted by the lady behind the counter:
'Don't worry he will be there.'

3.9

I feel a bit like Kenneth Williams in relation to my ex-colleagues, because the dead English comic actor's diaries revealed a man full of contempt and bitterness towards fellow performers, which was totally at odds with his jolly public persona.

We all have these 'dark thoughts' about others to a greater or lesser degree, it's just that most people are sensible enough not to publish them or don't get the opportunity to do so. Any comments I have made about former workmates are very mild and usually balanced by positive statements, sprinkled with plenty of self-criticism.

If I bump into any of them in the ancient and sporadically beautiful city of York I won't quite know how to behave, because I don't feel that much I've done is wrong. With time their over-reaction will settle down, and maybe one day Heather will finally bring herself to give me another hug. I suppose the simple act of leaving an office for good feels like some kind of betrayal to those who remain, without taking account of any of the other nonsense.

Because I've still not received my 'happy book' I had to contact the company concerned, pointing out that the volume in question was directed at those individuals suffering from stress and unhappiness, which their slow response was only making worse. The book outlet replied blaming supply problems – in other words they didn't have the book they claimed was in stock.

This Saturday morning in mid-November is more like Monday to Friday as I find myself completely alone again.

My daughter is staying at a friend's house, partner and son have gone to his swimming lesson in York, and Kazia is over in Bradford again. The mostly grey sky is showing the odd patch of blue, which I will take as a sign of brighter conditions ahead.

4

Talk of snow is clearly not the same as a real snowfall, yet we have had a miserable weekend of icy rain and plummeting temperatures. The usual culprits over Derbyshire way have had more genuine problems – the Snake Pass, Buxton, Matlock.

This Monday morning seems like it will never get light in the Yorkshire Wolds, and I don't expect Kazia will surface until midday. There is always the same consolation at this time of year – it is only just over one month until the shortest day, when very slowly it will begin to get light again.

Jonny phoned me first thing to say a few tiles had come off up at Muffin Heaven, but he'd heroically already replaced them. Thank God I can rely on a practical person to put right the cruel assaults of winter weather. It was interesting that he asked after Kazia as well, and I painted a delightful picture of a fragile Polish lass snuggled-up in the garage.

I've drunk too much wine and whisky over the weekend, which does bring temporary escape from harsh reality, but one always returns to the same bloated body and dangerous rut of negative thoughts. My positive thinking book will surely come this week, though it is no substitute for one of Heather's bear hugs.

On Friday I'm accompanying my daughter into York (school closed) for the first ice skating session of the season (I'll be watching). There is a realistic prospect of bumping into at least one ex-colleague, which is causing me a certain amount of anxiety, but on the other hand I don't feel ashamed of any recent actions – if properly understood.

As half-expected the local council have turned down our

application for a neon sign, which they feared might give the wrong impression about our establishment. I have now contacted a chap who carves traditional wooden signs from a tiny cottage out at remote Vessey Pasture – he was a little uncertain at first, but then gave a broad toothless smile that indicated his acceptance of the task.

4.1

Because of the high cost of heating oil it is always below the legal minimum temperature for office workers in our home, but it is impossible to be 'sent home' when you are already there. We will not be given the same permission as Muffin Heaven for wind power because we're too close to our jolly neighbours, and even the latest solar units are bound to struggle in northern England.

Perhaps the answer is for all villagers to use exercise bikes on a strict rota, meaning that all times of the day are covered, however I'm not sure if the six kilometres I've just completed will light more than a couple of light bulbs. We had a letter through the door last week telling us that there will be an interruption to electricity supply on Wednesday afternoon as part of the ongoing upgrade to our network. I hope this will help with the fairly regular power cuts that are experienced in this country location, particularly in winter.

I suppose there's been some improvement to my general fitness since starting this dull indoor biking, and my large trousers are falling down more – which is a good sign for me, and potentially amusing for other villagers. Adjusting my eating and drinking habits to bring them in line with rationing after the Second World War is proving much more difficult, as it's so easy to obtain nice things – you can even order food on the Web and have it delivered straight to the door.

During all the years of office work it was always difficult to keep leaving your desk for some stretching or walking, because you're paid to sit on your arse in front of a computer. At least now I can please myself about how long I sit down, and it's just a matter of personal motivation as to how much exercise is taken.

It will be good to have the walk up our big hill every morning to Muffin Heaven, and I'm keen to join the inscrutable Mr Wong for his T'ai Chi instruction. Just before I left the Civil Service Heather and Kate were considering dance classes, mainly for fitness, but in Kate's case to possibly meet a male life companion. I'm sure many men will want to dance with lovely Heather, and Kate is an attractive young thing herself.

There is no reason why we can't add dancing, poetry reading, fencing, and of course cooking to the programme at Muffin Heaven; it would be great to have the occasional gig too – Ron Sexsmith, Neil Young, Bruce Springsteen, maybe even Meat Loaf.

4.2

Emma said she'd been trying out a few recipes including cheese scones and the notoriously difficult Yorkshire Curd Tart, suggesting I should call in at her house on the way back from school with our young lad. Some good home baking was one way of relieving the hideous November gloom, apart from the daily ritual of lighting a real fire – something that most townies are no longer able to do.

'You can't beat a nice tart on a winter afternoon.'

'I don't know what you mean !' Emma replied laughing.

'Seriously, these curd tarts are excellent, not under-baked like some of those you can get in York.'

'I've had to throw plenty out before reaching a decent standard.'

'Gorgeous. Any chance of a cuppa ?'

'On its way, don't panic.'

Emma is in no way a beauty (like Heather), but she does have a pleasing, curvy figure and a pretty face – not forgetting short, raven-black hair, like some of the Icelandic women, and friendly dark brown eyes.

'Shut up you kids !'

'They do enjoy playing together.'

'Things are coming on well at the old barn then ?'

'At this rate we'll be ready to open long before April; and the sooner we can get some money into that till the better.'

'It'll be nice for me to get away from these four walls for a while.'

'You'll be very much needed – there's no way Kazia can cope on her own, and I don't think Jonny will fancy much cooking.'

We sat in contented silence for a while, apart from an occasional crash from the bedroom upstairs.

'Do you see anything of their father ?'

'You must be joking.'

'I haven't upset you ?'

'Not at all, we've all forgotten about that waster.'

'Thanks for the tea and tart.'

'You're not going anywhere till you try these cheese scones.'

'I'm in no rush to get back.'

4.3

As drier weather was promised on the coast I suggested to Kazia that she drive Jonny and me to Bridlington for a break from relentless preparations for Muffin Heaven. The morning rain in the Yorkshire Wolds was truly appalling, which made me yearn all the more for traditional fish, chips and mushy peas.

'Your car will be able to make it all the way ?'

'Good little car' Kazia said defensively.

I was happy to let Jonny sit up front and assist our Polish driver, just in case she was unfamiliar with our different road signs or priorities; also it would encourage their fledgling relationship to take flight.

'It's ages since I've been to Brid' said Jonny.

'Some parts have been renovated, but some seem unchanged since the 1960s.'

'I have not seen the sea in England' Kazia commented.

We took the so-called 'scenic route' via Sledmere, but the outer world did not look particularly inviting due to continued rain. Kazia and Jonny seemed happy enough in each other's company, making the odd comment about the weather or road conditions. She was rather incautious at roundabouts or junctions, tending to drive straight ahead without checking properly.

With it being November there was no problem getting a parking space right next to the harbour, though Kazia had a few problems reversing into a specific bay. It was not sunny, but the rain had disappeared, and it felt a few degrees warmer than recent bright, frosty days.

'The sea is very dark' said Kazia.

'It looks better in summer' I replied.

'Unless it's pissing it down !' Jonny laughed.

We walked along the mainly deserted north promenade towards the beach of sand and pebbles, where Jonny immediately tried to impress Kazia by attempting to skim stones across the fairly placid water. He was surprised when she demonstrated much greater skill at this pursuit, achieving an impressive ten bounces to his pathetic four.

There was no shortage of cafes and fish restaurants that could contribute to our growing knowledge on the subject, and perhaps boost the success of Muffin Heaven. Many were closed as it was low season, and many appeared to be in a sixties time warp, though some looked more crisp and modern. We found a fish and chip place overlooking the harbour, ordering three specials of large haddock, chips, mushy peas, tea, bread and butter.

'Pretty boats' Kazia observed.

'It must be a hard life searching for dwindling fish stocks' said Jonny.

The size of battered fish that arrived at our table was remarkably large considering all you hear about fishing industry problems, and it was a struggle for the friendly waitress to fit all three plates onto the small, shiny rectangle in front of us.

'I never eat all this.'

'Get stuck in' Jonny encouraged.

'This is the life' I said.

We slowly munched through the delicious feast, not feeling the need to make much conversation, and watching large seagulls soaring and swooping over the grey North Sea.

4.4

All is progressing remarkably well up at the old barn that is soon to be re-named Muffin Heaven, which shows it is possible to move forward without the positive thinking manual that had still not arrived. I have often repeated to myself since leaving the safety of office life: 'positive, modest, no inner negativity' - perhaps this has helped in some small way, along with the practical and now financial assistance of Jonny One-Thumb.

At the end of next week Mary is driving us over to the giant Swedish IKEA store beyond Leeds where they have fantastic bargains on cutlery, crockery and virtually everything else you might need for opening a smallish cafe. As always I'm looking forward to stuffing myself in their restaurant, which is usually extremely good value, though rather chaotic and lacking spirituality.

'You've still got some internal pointing on these stone walls then ?'

'It's quite time-consuming – this barn's bigger than you think.'

'At this rate we might be able to open late January, when the days are slowly getting lighter.'

'We need to get everything right, I don't want to rush.'

'Don't forget we'll both be getting pissed every day over Christmas and New Year, and not getting much done.'

'Are we planning any paintings or anything on the walls ?' Jonny wondered.

'Not sure whether to have a local wildlife theme using Robert Fuller's pictures, or lean towards symbols of Tibetan

Buddhism.'

'The folk round here will probably feel more comfortable with owls, hares and stoats.'

'Stoats are a very underrated animal.'

We sat quietly for a long time, not really making any final decisions, but just enjoying the western view over York's flat vale while sipping from large beakers of strong tea.

'How are you getting on with that Kazia then ?'

'Not bad.'

Jonny was a master of Yorkshire under-statement and had a wit drier than a Wolds valley bottom.

4.5

As if by magic, rather than the more prosaic means of Royal Mail delivery (much later in the morning than it used to be, if at all) my simple green and white happiness manual has arrived in the remote Yorkshire Wolds. I already feel it will be an essential part of the library loan section at Muffin Heaven, which can be returned again and again for the benefit of many sad bastards.

The Promised Land by Dr Rick Norris is 'A guide to positive thinking for sufferers of stress, anxiety, and depression'. The front cover shows a tiny desert island with giant palm trees, which must be the ideal way of life we all aspire to.

Having read the introductory and first chapter: 'Life – not for the faint hearted' I am already losing much of my scepticism because the book is written in such a simple no-nonsense style by a chap who has worked extensively as a psychologist in hospitals and the real world beyond. The only thing that's putting me off so far is the suggestion that effort is required to change our negative though patterns, and I'm not very good at effort.

For now I will keep the book hidden from my family as I fear (why fear ?) that they will not immediately understand my need to smash the outmoded mental structures of decades. It is very much NOT like having a stash of pornographic magazines under the mattress – I'm just going to place it on a bookshelf not often visited by Mary – until its move to Muffin Heaven library.

I have always sought the impossible love of someone like Heather to feel emotionally complete, yet this strategy has failed me spectacularly over the years. I will try to indulge in some self-love first, only much further down the line concerning myself with what others think or can provide.

Intellectually, this all sounds dandy, however the lack of contact from Heather and to a lesser extent Kate is hardening my heart even further – either that or leading to an eventual unravelling and disintegration of my entire being.

Today's weather has been very like my moods – starting gloomy and wet, then brightening for a brief time, now returning to heavy rain so I will get soaked when picking-up the young lad from school. Luckily, he is only six and not too old to give his weary dad a big hug, before we wander away from all the other gathered parents who are too old to remember the warmth and spontaneity of youth.

4.6

I am extremely fortunate to have the opportunity to forge a new life after so many years chained to a Civil Service desk, however there are many things I miss. Above all it has to be the lively conversation - when you're lucky enough to share an office where everyone gets on most of the time.

There were the silly things, like our magic puddle on the balcony that reliably informed us if it was raining and the intensity of rain. You can't always tell from simply looking out of the window if it's actually pissing it down, so the magic puddle would be invaluable as lunchtime or home time approaches. A simple pool of water on our third floor balcony was able to provide more accurate information than the most detailed weather forecast, and amusement for often-bored members of staff.

For a crude male human driven by the ever-powerful urge to reproduce I make no apology for the pinnacle of my inspiration at work – the many attractive women. Heather proved to be the most inspirational in all my working years, because however unkempt a gale or rain had made her travelling to our office she always made me say to myself: 'Wow ! She is beautiful.'

Until Muffin Heaven is established I am adjusting to a life where nobody comes in the morning and everybody leaves, so I must face up to all my uncertainties and my naked self with very few distractions. What will happen if our cafe gets no customers ? What if the roof blows off and we can't afford to replace it ? Will I end up homeless, living on the streets ? Will Heather ever get in touch ?

So I will reach for Dr Rick Norris to provide some

reassurance, but a book can be a very impersonal thing that is not capable of putting right all the imperfect nurturing of childhood and the inheritance of imperfect genes. I should remind myself more often that there are many people in this world with nothing, caught-up in horrendous wars or natural disasters.

Buddhists tell us that we can never find happiness by focusing on our own problems or trying to constantly improve our own material status – we should try to help others in need, give instead of take, take, take.

4.7

My visit into York on Friday coincides with the waxing full moon, and though I'll be keeping well away from my former office building it is quite possible I'll encounter an ex-colleague with feelings heightened by natural forces we barely understand. I have no scientific evidence, but colleagues and I did observe an increase in bizarre office behaviour as the moon was at its most powerful – so many Civil Servants rising like ocean waves to a climax of emotion.

In the Yorkshire Wolds we have the opportunity to be more in touch with the natural world, though sadly most people would rather tune-in to some nonsense on TV than observe the behaviour of barn owls.

'What do you think about an outside area of decking projecting over the Wold edge ?'

'Do we get enough warm days here to justify it ?' Jonny wondered.

'Even on cold days visitors could go out with some binoculars to watch birds or just absorb the view.'

'I'll get back in touch with the timber yard then' Jonny said reluctantly, bearing in mind the many other tasks he had to perform.

'Do you fancy a trip into York on Friday ?'

'Too much to do.'

I had hoped that Jonny would swell the numbers of our small party and offer some kind of protection if a difficult encounter occurred; this rift between ex-colleagues and myself has built-up in my mind, but for them it is probably just a matter or indifference or increased workload with staff leaving.

Again, it appeared we would never see light in the Wolds today, but nature always has its surprises for those willing to open their minds. I cannot consider another ride on my Velvet 250 motorcycle due to the still wet roads, because I am very much the fair weather biker waiting for perfect blue skies and warmth.

4.8

Christmas is only just over a month away and it is already having a minor impact on our project, as children and relatives start to make their greedy demands for presents or precious time. Kazia has informed she will be returning to Poland in mid-December and returning mid-January, while Jonny tells me he's off to stay with his brother in Shrewsbury for two whole weeks over the festive period.

We have made excellent progress with Muffin Heaven, which is after all one very large room – it's not like we're renovating an entire mansion or York Minster. I'm just worried about losing all this excellent momentum, but on the other hand I'm a big fan of celebrating at this darkest time of year, whether it be as a pagan, Christian, or one of the many other persuasions.

'It's a while since you've seen your brother then ?'

'He only got out of Shrewsbury a few months ago.'

'I thought you said he was living in Shrewsbury.'

'He is. I mean he came out of Shrewsbury prison.'

'You don't need to tell me what he did.'

'No secret. He got involved in a fight at Gay Meadow football ground.'

'That's been demolished hasn't it ?'

'It has now.'

'Did he get any unwanted attentions inside ?'

'Only one scuffle while playing table tennis apparently.'

My daughter has already insisted I order her the latest 'NOW' compilation of chart hits, and has also noted down the precise details of an expensive mobile phone she wants to replace her expensive mobile phone. When I was growing-up pop compilation LPs were not even sung by the original artists, so I suppose we have moved on in that respect.

The young lad has made an enormous list of presents from the enormous Argos catalogue, which gives the correct page number, code and general description for about twenty items he expects from friends and family. What has happened to the age of innocence when you were lucky to get a piece of fruit and an assortment of nuts ?

'Are you OK about Kazia going back ?'

'She's promised to phone.'

'I know she likes you.'

'How do you know ?'

'It's obvious.'

'Not to me.'

'Have you done it yet ?'

'I'm not answering that, you can bugger off home and do whatever you do on that bloody computer.'

4.9

'There's no way we can afford the outside decking area' Jonny said.

'Fuckin' hell, that would have really been the icing on the muffin.'

'If we make any money, then we can think about further developments.'

'Perhaps I can get Mary to landscape the western side and make a small garden ?'

'Why not ? We can still put chairs and tables out there in the summer. Aren't gardens supposed to face south though ?'

'Could we stretch to a water feature ? The sound of a fountain or waterfall is so therapeutic.'

'Don't get carried away – we'll ask Mary about the garden – any plants will have to be very hardy to survive in such an exposed location.'

'I don't know much about gardening, but maybe Alpine specimens would be suitable ?'

It was a genuine annoyance to lose the decked area that would have afforded even more spectacular views than the great west window, yet Mary has a true affinity with plants and will do an excellent job – if she agrees to get involved. Thinking about the large expanse of glass again makes me wonder if John Sentamu the splendid Archbishop of York might officiate at our opening. York Minster has such wonderful stained glass; and if we could stress that our cafe is as much a project to bring together the community as it is an eating-house.......

'I was out with Kazia last night.'

'And ?!'

'It wouldn't be right for me to give any details.'
'But all is well ?'
'Very well.'

5

We've had quite a few hits on the Muffin Heaven website already, including assurances that a number of people will definitely be visiting the remote Yorkshire Wolds and sampling our delights. Sadly, there have also been a small minority of what I can only describe as perverts who were clearly looking in the wrong place on the Internet.

I suppose we'll have to spend more money in the weeks before opening on adverts in the York Press, Gazette and Herald and Leavening Evening News. Jonny has been very generous with his financial and other contributions recently, so I might have to go begging to Mary for some cash.

Our wooden sign has been delivered by the old fella from Vessey Pasture, and it more than makes up for the disappointment over the planned neon advertising. We won't put it up outside for a while as people will probably think we're already open, and swear they can smell the aroma of baking muffins rising high above the Wolds. He has managed to achieve very clear and bold lettering by carving right through the wood and searing the edges black, which meant there was no need for the use of any paint.

Mary has all her gardening books out and is behaving like the Gertrude Jekyll of chalk horticulture, but she's extremely worried about the exposed and elevated site. She's been talking to a woman near Hunmanby who has opened her 'Wold garden' to the public for many years, though in a much more sheltered position.

It must be nearly Christmas as I've just taken delivery of a case of strong red wines, which will be difficult to keep from getting too cold in our draughty house.

'Mary.'

'Yes.' She continues reading her book.

'I hadn't thought about applying for a drinks license, what do you think ?'

'I suppose so.'

'You're not really listening are you ?'

'I'm trying to sort out this bloody garden.'

'Should we offer alcohol or not ?'

'People expect the option these days – if they're not driving.'

'We could even brew our own.'

'Now hang on, we've got more than enough to deal with already.'

5.1

As is so often the case my fears proved groundless – this time it was the terror of bumping into ex-colleagues intent on some kind of revenge, because I have gained a degree of freedom from office life. Instead we had a lovely day in York, blessed with brilliant blue skies and the excitement of Christmas only a few weeks away.

The main purpose of our trip was to allow my daughter and friend to skate on the ice rink at the Eye of York, which is a green area in front of the Castle Museum, Cliffords Tower and Crown Court. Their skating was fairly limited – most of the time being spent clinging to the sides or sliding a few yards before being hit by speed skaters.

I was very nervous as we looked around a few shops, ready to dive behind the DVD or novelty calendar shelves if a familiar face from my Civil Service past suddenly appeared. The calendar Nuns Having Fun caught my attention as I thought it might suit the humour of Jonny One-Thumb, though I only saw the front cover of nuns enjoying a garden swing – the other eleven months must be left to my warped imagination.

My daughter persuaded me to buy her an expensive pink mobile phone replacing the more expensive mobile phone I got her two years ago. Thank goodness the price of such items has dropped, and they now contain so many extra features like music player, flash camera, radio. I was reminded again of the simpler times of my youth when you were lucky to get a second-hand bicycle or a few chocolate gold coins.

It is still such a short time since I left the daily grind of office life (hardly work if you compare it with something like coal mining), yet it already feels as though the thirteen years were nothing and are a distant memory. The Muffin Heaven project has developed so quickly from a light-hearted conversation into a solid building that will soon breathe some much needed life into our rural community.

We watched our daughter and friend eventually show some competence on the ice by completing half a circuit of the compact arena – how lucky they are to be young and mostly carefree. It would be good to be thirteen again, skating a few yards then falling over in a heap of laughter.

5.2

Our Sunday newspaper had a supplement on baking with kids and contains a mouth-watering recipe for lemon and berry muffins. They say the key to success is to use fresh lemons and berries, and the secret is not to stir the mixture too much – it should be a little lumpy.

Kazia escaped from the garage to join us for a weekend fry-up.

'What do you think of the recipe ?'

'We can try tomorrow ? It look good.'

'We must get some fresh fruit first.'

'I go in car.'

'Enjoy your bacon and eggs first, there's no rush.'

'It was cold in garage last night.'

'We'll have to get the wood burners filled up before you go to sleep so the place stays warm.'

'It will be colder when I go back to Poland.'

'Jonny will miss you.'

Kazia smiled and her cheeks reddened slightly.

'I will bring back some special sausage.'

'I hope they don't seize it at Customs.'

'We all European Union now.'

'There are probably regulations on what a muffin must contain to be called a muffin.'

Kazia looked puzzled, and we finished our breakfast in silence, until the kids came in hitting each other with inflatable hammers.

'Do you miss being in Poland ?'

'Yes, but England more opportunity.'

'Like living in a freezing garage with no wages !'
'Exactly.'

5.3

Jonny was putting in a lot of work up at Muffin Heaven because he was aware of the long Christmas break now only a few weeks away. The place was pretty much an empty shell without any furniture or cooking equipment installed.

'We need to get those wood stoves installed and start drying this place out.'

'You can't deprive your Kazia of heating.'

'She can borrow a gas heater from me.'

'Why don't you ask her to move in with you ?'

'I don't think either of us is ready for that.'

'Maybe after New Year.'

Jonny went quiet for a while, and we just sat on some old crates looking through the giant west window over the grey, chilly Vale of York.

'I think I'm in love with her.'

'Steady on, you might burst a blood vessel !'

'I wish I knew exactly how she felt.'

'I've seen the way she looks at you – nothing to worry about, just give it some time.'

'I've never been that patient where women are concerned.'

'You're both going away for a few weeks so that should lend some perspective.'

'Suppose you're right.'

Jonny got up and started to fiddle with some lighting, so I wandered outside and left him to it. A kestrel was hovering over the grass verge, waiting for the right moment to drop on an unsuspecting small rodent.

5.4

The late November morning is finally emerging from a misty start, promising fairly warm temperatures after many dull and chilly days. I've already visited the market town of Malton for supplies as this has the nearest shops – six miles away. Perhaps we can offer some basics for locals at Muffin Heaven, like bread, milk, eggs, newspapers and magazines (make a note).

I had decided the weather was suitable for riding the Benelli Velvet 250, though there were quite a few slippery corners and mud dropped by tractors. Any lack of concentration could easily find you in a ditch, or even a dyke – and she wouldn't be too happy about it.

At the supermarket I noticed some chocolate and also blueberry muffins, but decided not to examine them closely as I had no expectation of anything remarkable. The main point of my journey was to stock up on bread, because despite a few recent trials with a bread-making machine the results are rather heavy and dense. I'll have to leave most of the baking and cooking to Kazia and Emma as my efforts are very hit and miss.

I have returned safely to our silent village, which surely must have buzzed with human activity many years ago before cars and the disappearance of most agricultural labourers. I've started reading a book: The Forgotten Landscapes of the Yorkshire Wolds, which attempts to trace changes to the countryside and human habitation from 1000 BC to the present day. There are some fascinating insights into an environment we often take for granted without fully understanding the many features of interest.

Kazia is not entirely happy with the removal of wood burning stoves, claiming that the single gas heater is both ineffective and soulless.

'We have no choice about getting the old barn dried out, I'm sorry.'

'I understand.'

'Would you consider staying with Jonny for a while ?'

'I don't think he want me.'

'You're wrong about that. Shall I have a word with him ?'

'Maybe after Christmas.'

'OK. I'll see if Mary has any extra blankets.'

Kazia and Jonny were displaying a degree of hesitancy that was exasperating, but Mary said it was best to let them find their own way.

5.5

I had a frantic phone call from Jonny saying a young man had turned-up at Muffin Heaven asking for me, and there was definitely something weird about him.

'What do you mean weird ?'

'I can't really talk, just get up here.'

'I'll be about ten minutes.'

As Kazia was off with friends again there was no quick way of climbing our steep hill towards the old barn; I didn't really know what to make of Jonny's tone because he didn't usually get flustered, and he'd given very little away.

'What's this fuss about then ?' I said opening the door.

'He's over there by the window.'

'Who is he ?'

'Says his name is Kunchen.'

'Kun what ?'

The smallish figure had his back to me, and all I could see was a shaved head with large protruding ears, that just went on staring out of the west window as I talked with Jonny.

'Has he said anything else ?'

'That he wanted to speak with you.'

I walked slowly over to the large expanse of glass and the young man turned to greet me with an enormous smile.

'My name is Kunchen.'

I could immediately see he was Tibetan despite a grey sweatshirt and jeans, and the very clear command of English.

'Can I help you ?'

'I have come from the east.'

'You mean Tibet ?'

'No, Driffield. The monastery near there.'

'I didn't know there was one. Would you like some tea ?'

'Yes please, I like the Yorkshire tea – better than our yak butter style.'

We sat down with Kunchen while he described his escape from the Chinese authorities in Tibet, and how his brother had died crossing the mountains with him.

'I must earn money to get back.'

'We have no jobs at the moment – maybe in a few months.'

'I cannot stay at monastery for long.'

'We already have one refugee staying in the garage at home ; I suppose you could bunk up here for a while and help Jonny.'

Kunchen smiled warmly. Jonny suggested we have a word outside.

'We can't afford all these hangers on.'

'You haven't complained about that attractive Polish lass.'

'No, but....'

5.6

Kunchen reminded us all, even Kazia, how relatively easy our lives can be in more fortunate countries – not by constantly banging on about his problems, but by a simple, radiant presence. Gradually, we discovered more and more, like the meaning of his name: 'all knowing', and the hardship of his family who were virtually starving in Tibet.

He didn't object to sleeping on the wooden floor at Muffin Heaven, and as we kept the wood burners on a low light throughout the night, if anything Kunchen was too warm. Jonny seemed very pleased with his new assistant, who never got in the way and always had some tea ready when most needed.

'I didn't know there was a monastery at Driffield' said Jonny.

'It is more of a big house with large garden.'

'These hills must seem very small to you ?'

'They are different, but still beautiful.'

'I don't know how soon we will be able to pay you anything.'

'This place will be success.'

'I wish I had your confidence.'

'Have you been to Tibet ?'

'No, but I went through Driffield on the train once.'

Kunchen seemed to appreciate Jonny's attempt at humour, and Kunchen's mysterious glow lit-up the old barn through the dark days of winter. There was much laughter and industry in the weeks before Christmas, as a gas-burning cooker and oven were installed, and there would be all the furniture to assemble when the lorry arrived from the Swedish outlet to the west.

5.7

I miss the daily lunchtime opportunity in my former life of wandering the ancient streets of York that usually found me behind the Minster, where it's possible to escape hustle and bustle – except in the height of summer when partially clothed people are strewn across the grass like discarded food wrappers.

There is still no word from Heather and Kate in particular, which suggests that all our office years meant nothing to them, while I made my usual mistake of attaching too much significance to our relationships. I wonder if they will even send me a Christmas card – not that these cards can be regarded as anything more than a commercial racket (in most cases).

My midday rambles gave the illusion of a social life because I was around so many people, yet I would only interact with those selling me sandwiches, a pasty, a coffee on the most superficial level. Now a trip into town is like a special treat or adventure; such is the quiet in our Yorkshire Wolds location that the sparrows now seem noisy, and as for the owl that starts hooting every day at dusk......

'Do you get snow here ?' Kunchen wondered.

'Sometimes – usually not much.'

'We get much snow in mountains.'

'Have you ever seen a snow leopard ?' I asked.

'No, they very shy.'

'We have loads of owls round here.'

'I listen to them at night.'

'Will you be able to go back to your family ?'

'I must go back.'

There hasn't been a spectacular and prolonged snowfall in the Wolds for many years, but I wondered if this winter might be different – with Kunchen here.

5.8

'Do you think we need a fancy coffee machine ? A Gaggia or something like that ?' I wondered.

'Ideally we would, but with finances as they are a decent filter coffee machine will have to do for now' Jonny replied. 'It feels more like we're running a hostel for waifs and strays at the moment.'

'I wouldn't be without Kazia and Kunchen.'

'Particularly Kazia.'

'Then there'll be Emma to pay as well once we get started.'

'We'll just have to rely on as much publicity as possible to generate visitors.'

'Kunchen was talking about some famous Tibetan coming over early next year.'

'Not the Dalai Lama ?'

'No, but Kunchen said he might visit us because he'd be staying at the Driffield monastery.'

'That might get the local press and TV interested, but who is he ?'

'Karmapa, I think he said.'

'Does Kunchen know him ?'

'Apparently they were boys together in Tibet and then met again at Dharamsala.'

We both became lost in our own thoughts for a while, staring out of the big west window at the enormous blue winter sky. Kunchen returned with a large basket of logs to feed the greedy stoves, and it felt like we were in the mighty Himalayas.

5.9

With just a few weeks to Christmas we were able to find small traces of innocence amidst all the commercial crap, mainly through our six year-old son and the annual play at the local primary school. These youngsters are perhaps more aware than any previous generation of all the toys and games available, yet there is still a simple magic in their performance of the Nativity, or this year's The Twelve Days of Christmas.

For a non-religious person like myself it's a relief to have a theme that is apparently not focused on Jesus Christ, and most people will take it that way, though some suggest that there may be hidden religious meaning in the carol. Our young lad has not yet divulged which part he'll be playing – most likely it will be one of the ten lords a-leaping, as he's usually incredibly hyperactive.

Secret rehearsals have been going on for several weeks, and it's remarkable that the majority of young children do keep quiet about what's happening, though most people will of course know The Twelve Days of Christmas from their own childhood.

Tomorrow we're going into battle at the heart of commercialism when Mary will drive us over to the giant IKEA store – an essential visit if we're to equip Muffin Heaven with cheap, but hopefully tasteful chairs, tables, crockery, cutlery etc. I dread to think how busy it will be so close to the winter holiday, but so long as I can get to the front of the restaurant queue.....

'What do you think about the Norden range of tables and chairs ?' Mary asked.

'Why do they always have these stupid names, like Billy bookcases or Lack shelving ?'

'Don't worry about that dear; the Norden is solid birch and has the simple look we're after.'

'I'm not paying sixty pounds for each bloody chair !'

'We can find some much cheaper than that, and the real bargains will be kitchen utensils and so on.'

'I'm really looking forward to it.'

'Cheer up, I know how much you love shopping' said Mary laughing.

6

Before Kazia returned to Poland for the Christmas season she went for a farewell meal with Jonny at the Bay Horse, Burythorpe. The pub had recently been done up to match many of the other eating places that had turned their backs on the traditional drinking den in favour of posh country dining.

'I'm not really used to this sort of place' said Jonny, who looked slightly uncomfortable in jacket and tie.

'It is very nice.'

He began to feel a little more relaxed as he saw Kazia's warm smile and the beautiful eyes that were so wide open and vulnerable.

'I will miss you.'

'It is only a few weeks.'

'I'm not looking forward to seeing my brother again.'

She placed a reassuring hand on Jonny's arm, and they maintained eye contact for what seemed like an eternity.

'You are enjoying the meal ?' asked the waiter.

'Lovely' replied Jonny.

'You could maybe come with me to Poland next time.'

'I'd like that.'

There were only a few other people in the pub, and the atmosphere was very peaceful except for the occasional crack and spit of logs in the enormous fireplace. Jonny found it hard not to stare at Kazia as she slowly munched through some roast pheasant, and shadows of flame licked her cheeks.

'Can I stay with you tonight ?' she asked suddenly.

Jonny struggled to remain composed, feeling a dramatic rush of excitement throughout his body.

'Of course.'

6.1

'You look pleased with yourself considering Kazia's gone.'
'I'm looking forward to seeing my psycho brother in Shrewsbury.'
'How did the meal go ?'
'Good.'
Jonny One-Thumb was not keen to divulge any details of what had really happened between himself and Kazia, preferring to revel in the elated feelings that flowed from the night they'd spent together. Kunchen was helping to put together the IKEA tables and chairs, and was making good progress without once referring to the instructional diagrams.
'All seems to be going very well up here.'
'Perhaps we can think about opening late January ?' Jonny wondered.
'Karmapa come Driffield 1st February' said Kunchen.
'Do you think he could come here to open Muffin Heaven on Saturday 2nd ?'
'I find out.'
'If not we'll have to get the Krankies' Jonny said.
'I think comedy has moved on since their heyday.'
While Kunchen and Jonny slowly and cheerfully worked their way through all the boxes of furniture, I gazed out of the west window across the misty Vale of York. With binoculars I might have been able to see the large former office building containing Kate and beautiful Heather, but still having heard nothing from them it was best to focus on Christmas over indulgence, swiftly followed by final preparations for our grand opening.

I haven't progressed very far with the positive thinking book – not because I've become depressed – simply that I've managed to keep dark thoughts at bay by trying to dismiss any negative tendencies and trusting in a bright future for Muffin Heaven. Kunchen says it will be a success, and that is good enough for me, even though a Tibetan Buddhist's measure of good fortune might be vastly different from our own.

6.2

Today is a mild, damp December day, and also a slight break from routine because our six year-old son has such a bad cold he must remain at home. Normally he is literally dragged from bed just after seven in the morning, but today he's still sleeping at eight-thirty. Any preparations for the school production of Twelve Days of Christmas must be forgotten for this day of rest and watching kids TV.

It seems strange not to have a young Polish woman living in the garage, which I would recommend to any family possessing a well-built 'room' attached to their home. It is clear from Jonny's cheerful demeanour that they shared more than a meal the other night, but I'm happy to let him think nobody else knows.

I'm not sure if Kunchen has anywhere to go over the Christmas holiday, but he will be welcome to share the vegetable part of our festive fayre. He has been telling me a little more about the man we hope will be opening Muffin Heaven – the 17th reincarnation of the Gyalwa Karmapa. Apparently there has been much dispute over who is the genuine Karmapa, but the one visiting Yorkshire is backed by the Dalai Lama.

Kunchen has proved to be a delightful character who quietly and busily will undertake any task from constructing furniture to cleaning out the bogs. I wouldn't fancy spending so many nights alone in the old barn, but he doesn't seem to care whether there is human company or not. His life so far has clearly been so difficult that the basic conditions on top of the Wold are no challenge to his open-hearted and hardy personality. Many lesser beings would have become embittered and self-centred, yet Kunchen's Buddhist faith shines like a beacon across the winter hills.

'You'll be off soon yourself Jonny.'

'I'm a little apprehensive about meeting my brother after so long.'

'Is he the aggressive type ?'

'He can be after a few drinks.'

'Good job we don't associate Christmas with drinking then.'

'Very amusing.'

'You can see the new Shrewsbury Town football stadium !'

'If I can drag him out of the pub.'

6.3

As we are less than two months from the designated date of opening I thought it would be a good idea to erect the Muffin Heaven sign outside with the hope of attracting some passing interest. Jonny said he would also set-up a light sensitive beam focused on the sign that would illuminate throughout the long dark hours of December and January.

'Can you get the sign up before you go to Shropshire ?'

'Do you want it fastened to the wall or swinging like a traditional pub one ?'

'If it's swinging it will be visible from both road directions.'

'We'll need lights each side and a metal bracket, but it shouldn't be too difficult. To be honest I don't mind delaying my trip for a day or two.'

'I'm sure everything will be fine; you don't want to risk getting caught in a Christmas Eve snowfall.'

'If it snows on Christmas Eve and is still laying on Christmas Day will the bookies pay-out for a white Christmas ?'

'You must be joking – those money-grabbing bastards !'

We were approaching the record for the mildest December temperature, which made talk of snow somewhat bizarre; climate change experts said it would more likely be heavy rain and flooding rather than the white stuff all children pray for.

'Have you heard from Kazia ?'

'We text everyday.'

'You're more like a couple of teenagers – at least she is, in terms of age.'

'God bless Viagra !'
'Get yourself off to Stubbs for a wall bracket.'
'I will try to keep my mind on DIY.'

6.4

As we approach the celebration of Christmas, more significant for me is the shortest day that is a few days before; is it a mere coincidence that we have Christ's birth and the darkest time of the year at roughly the same time ? I know that most people in this country have no interest in religion and will value much more the painfully slow lengthening of days towards spring and summer.

This December morning is still fairly dark at eight-thirty with vast grey clouds moving slowly north-east; again I will have a small companion today, as our son is not recovered from the bad cold, and was tossing and turning between bad dreams all night. Yet somehow he is already up, dragging toys from the cupboards and coughing like a beagle that has smoked forty cigarettes every day for years in a hideous scientific trial.

'The winds won't be doing my garden any good' said Mary.

'You can get it all sorted in the spring.'

'But you're opening at the beginning of February.'

'Nobody will notice, they'll be more concerned about getting inside for a hot drink.'

'And a muffin.'

'And a muffin.'

Heather suddenly came into my mind – the person who first planted the seed of Muffin Heaven. In my last few weeks at the office she would bring her tiny daughter past the window every morning and a frantic few moments of waving would ensue. I feel sad that these fleeting times of innocence have been lost, replaced by probably not even a Christmas card.

Perhaps Heather, Kate and other former colleagues will be inspired by our grand opening to set any differences to one side and travel into the chilly Yorkshire Wolds. They might realise that there is a good life beyond the dusty Civil Service, and surely humans have a greater purpose than sitting behind a desk for decades of their working lives.

6.5

If I could visit the giant store IKEA on a daily or even weekly basis without taking advantage of the cheap fried breakfast it would not be long before I returned to the healthy physique of youth. On last week's trip we must have walked several miles, particularly as Mary wandered off, which resulted in much extra legwork trying to locate her.

I have since got into a time-wasting dispute with the company due to the purchase of an Indian rug advertised in one part of the store at 69 pounds, but when we checked the receipt at home they'd charged us 75 pounds. After contacting customer services via the Internet Leeds IKEA have denied any knowledge of this pricing, though Mary and I remain convinced they made the mistake. I would be interested to know how much the local Indian workers are paid for these marvellous rugs; our six quid is not really the point – more the common occurrence in supermarkets and other large outlets of charging more at the till than the price displayed.

I am slightly sweaty after a session on the exercise bike that must be having some positive effect, though certainly not dramatic. With the Christmas eating and drinking season approaching there is unlikely to be any reduction in my weight; I should bear in mind that we have already booked a holiday to the Greek island of Samos next year and it's essential to look respectable in a tight swimsuit. My mum has informed us of an article in the usually reliable Guardian that refugees from Africa are first going to Turkey and then crossing the few miles to Samos – so we may find the place overrun by unofficial entrants to the EC.

Our young lad is quietly watching a Batman video sandwiched between two IKEA blankets; I should point out in the interest of balance that for every soft toy IKEA sell at this time of year one pound is donated to helping poor children around the world. We purchased two largish rats at only £1.99 for our brats - these cute (real) creatures had featured in the TV programme I'm A Celebrity Get Me Out Of Here, which had the family transfixed over recent weeks. It was great to see the endearing gay Panto-star Christopher Biggins crowned queen of the jungle, because of his constant good humour and delightful nature.

If the Karmapa pulls out of our grand opening we could always consider Biggins, though now his career is so boosted by enduring the challenges of jungle life there is little chance we could afford his services. It must be fantastic to be paid a great deal of money simply to amuse people with your personality, and there is even talk of him replacing the UK chat host institution Michael Parkinson with a show that will doubtless be called Biggins.

I may have to try on some summer clothing later as the weather is so incredibly mild for December, despite the enormous black cloud slowly drifting over this peaceful Yorkshire Wolds village.

6.6

Emma called round looking rather grim-faced for a usually cheerful young lass, and I invited her in for a cup of tea.

'What's the problem ?'

'It's about the cafe.'

'Yes ?'

'I won't be able to work there.'

'That's a shame, why not ?'

'I've started taking some kids while the parents are at work.'

'You mean childcare.'

'Yes, but I'm not registered yet.'

'Well, that's a real shame, but we have got Kunchen as well now.'

'Kun who ?'

'A lovely Tibetan chap.'

'Can we still come to visit at the cafe ?'

'Of course, it'll be a lovely walk up the hill for you on a fine day.'

I was a little disappointed as it's always nice to be surrounded by women, but could fully understand why Emma was entering the lucrative world of childcare – not that it's easy looking after today's spoilt brats.

'We're opening early February, so any time after that you'll be more than welcome.'

Emma started to cry.

'There's no need for that.'

'I've let you down.'

'No, you need to earn some money, and you're great with

kids.'

Her face brightened like the winter morning sun finally rising above sheer chalk valleys.

6.7

We have come so far in a short time, but are like mountaineers below the summit of Everest, because many do not make it all the way and are forced back by terrible weather, or even die trying to attain their goal. Because of all the help received and help that will come in the future there is a good chance Muffin Heaven will be a success, but we cannot know for certain – in human life there will always be this uncertainty.

I was very moved by a television programme last night: The Secret Millionaire, which featured a secret millionaire ! A very rich property owner went undercover as a simple hospital volunteer, establishing who was most in need of financial assistance. It was very revealing to see how much the National Health Service is dependent on the input of unpaid volunteers, allowing nurses and other staff to perform more technical tasks.

At the end of the programme he presented cheques to a cancer support group, a stroke support group, and some individual carers who were coping in very tough circumstances. They were all shocked and tearful to find that the apparently very ordinary bloke was actually a successful businessman willing to provide cash input.

He appeared to have learnt a great deal himself from helping with the most basic tasks on a hospital ward, like feeding those who might otherwise go without or changing soiled sheets. I can only hope that the millionaire will continue to help others financially, and perhaps more importantly on a physical and emotional level. If all those who are well-off shared their wealth and time more freely it would be a much happier and fairer society.

We are hoping that Muffin Heaven will be a boost to the sometimes difficult and isolated lives of our rural community, because the main aim is not to get rich, though we will need to make some money to survive. It will be our policy never to turn anyone away who is not dressed appropriately, or for any other reason except that the visitor is aggressive or unpleasant.

I would dearly love to be a benefactor to those in need, both financially and otherwise, but it will take an awful lot of individual acts of generosity to create a happier world. Charitable acts can never really be a substitute for a fairer society; currently vast amounts of wealth remain concentrated in the hands of a relatively small minority.

Somebody get me a strong coffee with a fresh muffin........... I'm feeling rather weary as the season of goodwill approaches.........

6.8

I wish it were possible to record every detail of my dream about Heather last night, yet as always the often bizarre strands of storyline fade so quickly from the conscious mind. I am keen to regain as much as possible because dreams are currently the only arena in which to encounter my beautiful ex-colleague.

At least this December morning is bright and cold, killing-off any strawberry plants or daffodils that have been reported growing prematurely on the local TV news. The weather is not extreme enough to distract me from Heather's beauty, and even to believe that we might meet again in a positive way.

The curiosity aroused by the opening of Muffin Heaven will be too much for some former workmates to bear, who will come if only in the hope of seeing me fail. Heather has more about her than that – not the type to waste time wishing for the failure of others – she has a fair-minded and caring side.

Am I falling into the same trap that has ensnared me so often through this uneventful life ? To project higher qualities upon physically attractive women than could ever exist in reality, leading to inevitable disappointment after years of unfulfilled fantasy.

I must get out in the cold morning air, because the simple act of walking can do much to clear a trouble mind - looking beyond one's own petty concerns at the birds foraging for scarce winter food, stoats dancing to confuse their prey, owls snoozing until the early December dusk. I love listening to the hypnotic sound of our small village brook, that never stops flowing in the driest summer, bringing life to our community blessed with many natural gifts.

'I'm going to work now' Mary shouts.

'See you later.'

Mary is a practical person, a methodical woman, with little interest in dreams or any other nonsense. Now I am truly alone, facing my raw self and all its imperfections. At least now I can climb the steep hill to the old barn, which is becoming a real means of basic human engagement.

6.9

'Isn't it time you buggered off to Shrewsbury to see your brother ?'

'I'm still undecided.'

'He's your brother for fuck's sake !'

'What does buggered mean ?' Kunchen asked.

'In this context it means to go away' Jonny replied helpfully.

'And fuck ?'

'Where is he staying ?' I persisted.

'They've found him a bedsit.'

'Can't be much fun at this time of year.'

'I'll go, it's just that our relationship has never been easy.'

'You've been working so hard up here with Kunchen – you both deserve a break.'

'Next you'll be telling me there's more to life than Muffin Heaven.'

'We're only talking about a short break; Kunchen will be coming down to stay with us as well.'

'Whatever.'

I made some tea for Jonny and myself, opening a fresh packet of chocolate digestives; Kunchen seemed happy with just a glass of spring water. The mood changed from one of mildly confrontational to vaguely cheerful, mainly due to the positive vibes that always came from our Tibetan companion. Our kids had half-forgotten about the idea of getting a Tibetan Terrier, Tibetan Spaniel or some other hound as they thoroughly enjoyed mucking about with Kunchen – an endlessly patient and loyal friend.

'I'll drive down tomorrow then.'
'The forecast is good.'

7

This feels like such a strange time after all the activity of recent weeks, and with Kazia and Jonny away sharing their own family problems and joys. Mary has given me a long list of presents I'm supposed order on the Internet, though we're fast running out of postage days, and all our money has been invested in the bizarre project of Muffin Heaven.

There is a stormy feel to the weather – Saturday didn't get light at all, with hideous rain all day. On the way back from York we had a puncture in the middle of nowhere, called the RAC breakdown and waited for a long time in darkness with only the hazard warning lights casting feeble illumination on the muddy grass verge. We were lucky that a fellow villager turned up and changed the wheel for us, because I lack much practical skill and the breakdown van was attending more urgent calls.

We are promised plummeting temperatures this week, and I still find magic in lighting a real fire most days, which cannot be compared to flicking the central heating switch as a means of creating genuine warmth and atmosphere. I can see the front garden vegetation is taking a battering from vicious wind, and the many sparrows attempting to shelter and survive seem particularly noisy at the moment.

I shouldn't care that I will receive and send not a single Christmas card this year, but having attempted to contact some of my former colleagues without a response it is not for me to make another approach now. My visit to the school's production of Twelve Days of Christmas should provide some diversion from these days without much happening at Muffin

Heaven, and most family and friends away.

'You will be happy to stay with us for the next few weeks Kunchen ?'

'You very kind.'

'It has been a pleasure for us to have you at the barn.'

'I have liked it up there.'

'I'm sure Kazia won't mind you taking over in the garage for a while, it's quite cosy.'

'I am used to living simple.'

I wish that Mary wasn't so keen to spend money we hadn't got on all kinds of gifts that might be discarded anyway, but she and the kids are incapable of following the fine example of our Tibetan guest.

7.1

With even Kunchen away from Muffin Heaven there was a real pleasure for me in savouring the atmosphere up there alone after the physical struggle of climbing up our steep hill. I had got used to the black Labrador barking loudly and persistently when passing the lonely property on the way towards our old barn – the old fella had assured me that his bitch wouldn't bite.

I liked it best when the sky had cleared after heavy rain and it was possible to see way beyond York towards more undulating countryside and ultimately the mighty Pennines. Our large west window was surely a wise investment, and we had now arranged most tables and chairs to enjoy at least some of the magnificent view.

'Anybody there ?'

I opened the heavy wooden door to see an old cyclist in a bright yellow jersey.

'Are you open ?'

'Not yet, but you can come in for a cuppa if you like.'

'I've just had a hard ride up from Kirby Underdale; did you know the Post Office had closed there ?'

'They've closed in most villages round here.'

I made the old chap a strong cup of tea and put a few biscuits out.

'Very decent of you.'

'You do a fair bit of cycling then ?'

'I've been riding the Wolds since the 1950s – some parts haven't changed much.'

'We're hoping to get quite a few ramblers and cyclists in here.'

'When do you open ?'

'Early February.'

'I'll put the word about in the cycling clubs.'

I watched the old bloke sipping his tea and marvelled at how a man clearly over seventy could cope with some of the gradients round about.

'Don't tell me you managed to bike from Kirby up to the top road ?'

'Came through Uncleby, but it's just as steep.'

'I'll have to trade in my motorbike for a pushbike.'

'You could lose a few pounds young 'un.'

We both laughed loudly, enjoying the tea and simple chat.

7.2

Another afternoon up there it was heavy, icy rain and you couldn't see more than a few hundred yards with cloud so low on the tops; inside the stone barn was nice and snug with one of the wood burners giving out plenty of dry heat. The Birdsall estate had given us a couple of bottles of bourbon because of the business we'd put their way, and no doubt hoping for more next year - I took one out from the secret stash along with a small tumbler.

I suppose it's easier drinking than some of those Scottish single malts that can blow your brains out with the taste of raw nature, but particularly pleasant to sip in the depths of winter. I had much more time for reading since leaving the office job, and my latest was Betty Blue that I'd only just started really. I was intrigued to read the original story having seen the extremely erotic and tragic French film in the early eighties, and was already enjoying the author's fairly straightforward style.

So I sat in the mostly finished barn reading the sexy cult novel, drinking whiskey, listening to the wild weather lash the Wold top. I wished that we didn't have to welcome any customers to Muffin Heaven, just keep the place as a private refuge from the pressures of the modern world. Sadly there was no chance of that, unless we were all going to get jobs doing something very different – there remained an urgent need for money.

It was very satisfying to look round the building that was a shell not so long ago and see all the work (mostly by Jonny) that had been completed - even with one thumb missing it's possible to overcome many challenges and create the potential of a vibrant business. There was still the possibility that all our endeavours might not pull the punters in, but even in the worst-case scenario we could make a substantial profit by selling it as a house.

When my eyes started to droop a little I put the radio on for the afternoon play, thinking what a fortunate life it was compared to the mind-numbing paper shuffling of Civil Service existence. I'd already drunk half a bottle of the delightful bourbon and all felt kind of surreal because of being so far from other humans and the thick cloud which seemed to contain and push any thoughts back into the stone building.

I'm not sure how long I'd been asleep, but it was very dark when I woke in the warm barn with a tiny amount of light coming from the stove that had almost gone out. I didn't feel fearful or uncomfortable sitting alone with all the empty Wolds beyond, just grateful to have enjoyed a few hours of precious solitude.

The sky had cleared as I dropped down the steep hill towards the village and home; city lights were far away to the west, while countless stars crowded the chill night sky that promised a hard frost next morning.

7.3

What else is there for a family to do on a wet day before Christmas other than to visit a designer outlet or similar indoor shopping mall ? We all went to the one near York (including a bemused Kunchen), which is located on the site of a former mental hospital. I stayed there myself more than twenty years ago after a nervous breakdown, enduring a few months of treatment including three sessions of electro-convulsive therapy.

There can be very few now remembering what used to go on in the old hospital, like a Nazi concentration camp being replaced by a burger outlet – though many relics of the Second World War have been preserved to ensure we do not forget the hideous cruelty perpetrated by cowards.

It took a long time to find a parking space because of all those looking for festive bargains, but sadly the place was not full and we were sucked into the building of bright and flashing lights. Kunchen had a problem with the automatic doors and escalator, and people seemed to stare at him despite the fact he was dressed in ordinary jeans and jumper.

He looked rather shell-shocked as we found an uncleared table in the food hall, and refused to have anything to match our kids' choices from McDonalds; Mary and I went for the slightly more adventurous Pizza Hut Express, which even included a large salad. Hundreds of noisy people battling to the front of food queues and fighting for table space was disturbing enough to me, but it was the first time I had seen Kunchen without a smile.

The highlight of my visit (apart from driving away) was

finding the film of Betty Blue on DVD for only four pounds
! I will have to ensure that it is viewed when Mary and the
kids are out because of the erotic and later disturbing content.
Our young lad seemed happy enough with a plastic boat we
bought him for a few pounds – Mary let the side down by
purchasing some expensive leather biker-style boots.

The December day just refused to get light and persistent
rain created giant puddles at the roadside; Kunchen was much
happier just watching the appalling weather, and went back to
the car some time before we'd completed a circuit of all the
glittering shops.

'You didn't enjoy that ?' I asked him.

'In Lhasa the Chinese are making many shops, but not like
this.'

'We won't make you go to any more.'

It was a relief to see Kunchen smile again, bringing some
genuine warmth to such a bleak winter day.

7.4

I was on the exercise bike when my mobile phone performed its frog croak announcing a caller at such an inappropriate moment.

'Hello.'

'Do you have any girls available ?'

'I'm sorry ?' My own heavy breathing.

'Do you have anyone available for tonight ?'

'What are you talking about ?'

'Is that Muffin Heaven ?'

'Yes.'

'Can you help me then ?'

'We're a cafe, and we don't open till February.'

'I can't wait that long.'

The chap hung up, and I returned to my daily low-impact cycling that always has the same view out of our dining room window. I hate being disturbed on the bike because I'm so keen to get the tedious routine over, and it's particularly annoying when a time-waster's on the line.

The view from our window today is a clear blue sky and frosty conditions; the local TV weatherman was foolish enough last night to suggest that there might be snow on Christmas Day, but admitted it was far to early to offer any certainty to the millions of romantics around the United Kingdom.

The phone croaked again.

'Hello.'

'It's Jonny.'

'How's your brother ?'

'No fights yet.'

'I've just had some idiot on the line looking for girls !'
'What did you say ?'
'That we are a cafe not yet open.'

7.5

We were assembling the core of a decent collection of paperbacks for our little library at Muffin Heaven, which would have to operate the policy of either loan to bring back, or take one and leave one. The only danger with this is that we'll probably end up with loads of Harold Robbins and John Grisham as all our more soulful stuff is gradually robbed. Kunchen was rather puzzled by the process as he could neither read English nor had he come across many books at all during his youth.

The most recent addition I'd added was the very enjoyable History of Tractors in Ukrainian, which is not an agricultural manual – mainly focusing on the hopeless marriage of an old man to a young, busty woman, and the tragi-comedy that ensues. I found it slightly difficult to get into the rhythm of (more my fault than the book's), but as it progressed I wished for the story to go on and on. I don't know if the author is planning a follow-up or even a so-called prequel, but it's certainly a unique combination of comedy and serious themes.

Another great read from recent times is The No.1 Ladies' Detective Agency series of books, which follows our unlikely lady heroine becoming a private detective in Botswana. As with the Tractor book this immediately establishes a unique, and for most unfamiliar, environment for the adventures to unfold. At heart they are just damn good stories that appeal to a wide range of people; in the example of our lady detective it also has the added dimension of her being a decent person attempting to right some of the many injustices found in Africa.

I think we will have to shock people by including some slim volumes of poetry, which are barely read in many countries of the world despite their enormous importance (in some cases !). What can be fascinating about poetry is that so much can be said in so few words – in the best examples a couple of lines might be just as powerful as one thousand pages of prose.

This makes me think of The Little Prince, which many might dismiss as a book for children, but contains more insight and magic than ninety-nine percent of the trash published these days.

'All these books' said Kunchen. 'What are they for ?'

'Sometimes simply for pleasure, but many deal with important themes like love, death, religion.'

'I have only studied the Buddhism.'

'We have a rather different, more commercial approach to things here.'

'I've heard of your Harry Potter.'

7.6

I have just experienced the social highlight of my Christmas calendar (I won't be invited anywhere else), which was the much anticipated school production of Twelve Days of Christmas. Because I'm currently at home in the daytime I've attended the lesser matinee performance – Mary will be going to the main evening production.

Just like the days when I was a pupil - a seat at the back of the hall or class was my only goal, which was achieved by sitting on some fairly sturdy desks, rather than the small chairs that surely would crumple. I was also lucky to be next to a nice lady whose fat husband left her for another woman in Scarborough, and we exchanged a few words before the show began.

On entering the school a couple of kids relieved me of one pound, which they claimed was for some competition; then a large neighbour took two pounds off me for the raffle. There were a few familiar faces and a jolly atmosphere, so I didn't feel the complete social outcast that is my true vocation.

I was pleased to see in the programme that one of the main characters was played by Ted Hughes – a famous English poet who has been dead for some years. My own lad was listed under Drummers, but for some reason there was a category called Hoop-La consisting of five young girls. Most of the other groups made sense: Lords, Ladies, Maids, French Hens etc.

These things always seem to go on longer than a numb backside would wish, but at least some enthusiastic parents could photograph and film their youngsters in bright costumes.

There were a few difficult moments when older kids had to speak or sing alone, but these were quickly followed by loud pop music and bizarre dancing. Loud applause of relief and appreciation ended the show, and who could not be moved by their mostly innocent endeavours? Typically, my lad was warned for mucking about with another drummer, and later separated from his group altogether – something that might have a lasting detrimental effect on his development.

The children went back to classrooms to get changed and the eagerly awaited raffle began with numbers that bore no relation to the three lines I was holding. My patience was rewarded with the perfect gift of a bottle of twelve year-old Glenlivet – sadly only a half-bottle, but very welcome anyway.

I collected my young boy, still wearing a black moustache above his top lip, along with the school Christmas pudding we'd ordered; in just a few minutes after the show he'd managed to make one lad cry and stolen the boxing gloves from some other poor sod. We took the short cut back over the fields, hoping to avoid any angry parents, relieved to close the front door and put the heating on immediately.

7.7

If I were still in the office, today is the occasion of the Christmas dinner – I know this because I actually chose the venue before leaving the grey world of the Civil Service. As things have turned out it's a good job I elected not to go due to the great wall of silence that has been erected by former colleagues, despite my few attempts to contact them. There are a small minority of workmates who will genuinely get on and fully enjoy eating together, but most will merely pretend to have a good time, and senior managers will firmly stick together offering the occasional polite gesture to their inferiors. It always amused me how the women would slap on more make-up than usual for this annual outing and bring out the extra special outfit just purchased in a pre-Christmas sale – they seem to confuse natural beauty with the fake variety that is never convincing.

Our village is very frosty this morning with a severe wind chill factor, yet I can find more comfort here than in a working environment that depends upon people lying to each other about their level of mutual hatred so the 'team' can get the job done. I am genuinely sad not to have the opportunity to get pissed with Kate, Heather and a few other decent folk, but the severance has been more sudden and complete than expected.

I suppose this break with the past is a necessary part of succeeding in our new venture, when we hope many new faces will be coming through our big front door. Most will just be passing trade that will never become part of the fabric of Muffin Heaven, but there will be some peculiar souls that will find and provide comfort in our cosy old barn.

'You seem a bit quiet this morning' Mary observed.

'Too much Glenlivet last night.'

'See you later then.'

'Have a good day at work.'

I could think of nothing better to do on a bright and frosty morning than climb to the Wold top and along to Muffin Heaven, where I planned to try out our new equipment with some recipes that would blow the winter socks off any unexpected rambler or cyclist who knocked on the door.

7.8

My heart wasn't in the mixing bowl, partly because I was slightly hung over from the excellent Glenlivet and partly because the pale face of Heather was still haunting me like a sensual ghost. I didn't have Kazia or Jonny to distract me from thoughts that were proving more difficult to dismiss than expected; I kept wandering to the big west window and gazing across the misty Vale of York.

'Hello !' I recognised the cheerful voice of Emma.

'Good to see you !'

'We all decided to go for a walk – it was bloody hard pushing a buggy up that hill.'

I made her a coffee and found some juice for the kids.

'This place is looking great.'

'It's mainly down to Jonny's hard work.'

'The childcare is going OK, but it's a shame to miss out on this.'

'I'm finding it a little too quiet at the moment.'

'Christmas disrupts everything.'

'What are you doing this year ?'

'Going to my mum's in Malton - we always like to have a family war over the Turkey.'

'Sounds like fun !'

'I just don't get on with my sister.'

'That's a shame.'

I was pleased that Emma had turned up to snap me out of the mood I was slipping into, and with the little ones running madly about the place it felt like we were already open for business.

'If I don't see you before the big day, have a good Christmas.'

'And you. We'll see you for the opening I hope ?'

'Of course.'

Emma gave me a friendly hug, which was quite different from those terrifying bear hugs that Heather always used to perform.

Joe Hebden

7.9

'What the fuck are you doing back ?!'
'It was no good, we just couldn't get on.'
'The poor bugger's fresh from jail, surely you could offer a bit more support ?'
'It's always been the same, ever since he smashed up my bike when I was five.'
'That was quite some time ago !'
Jonny fell silent, and I didn't know what else to say, so wandered off to the kitchen to make a pot of tea – what else can you do in a minor crisis ?
'You might as well try one of these grape and banana muffins – I'm not sure if they work.'
'Thanks.'
'So what exactly happened ?'
'We went for a curry in the centre of Shrewsbury.'
'Sounds innocent enough.'
'He got into a fight with some gobby young lads who'd had too much lager – the Korma was flying everywhere.'
'Did the Police come ?'
'I managed to get him out just before they arrived.'
We both bit into the experimental muffins and were unable to speak for a few minutes.
'That recipe could be a bit dodgy.'
'Not quite the classic blueberry' said Jonny.
'Perhaps you can try again with him in the New Year ?'
'He'll probably be back inside by then.'
'Of course you're welcome to join us for the giant turkey; it'll be a bit quiet for you till Kazia gets back.'
'I'll think of something to do.'

8

We are incredibly lucky to have the prospect of one of the major figures of Tibetan Buddhism – Karmapa – to open our humble barn, if he doesn't pull-out at the last moment (like the lorry driver hoping to avoid a child). But it's our local Archbishop of York who is again capturing the news headlines with dramatic gestures and comments that will inspire Christians and non-Christians alike. Most recently he has cut up his dog collar on live TV, saying that he won't wear one again until the terrible tyrant Robert Mugabe relinquishes power in Zimbabwe. What a splendid chap our Archbishop is.

With so many problems in the world it is easy to overlook the plight of mild-mannered Tibetans who have suffered so much at the hands of Chinese Government brutality. I always like to make the distinction between the vile acts a Government and their army might commit, and the population in general, who if led by a more benevolent force would doubtless follow their good example.

The current incarnation of the Dalai Lama is an admirable and sensible man who realistically does not demand complete independence from China, just to allow Tibetans autonomy and self-expression within a larger Chinese framework – even though an independent Tibet would be fully justified based on historical evidence.

We can only hope that the Olympics soon to be hosted by China will bring about a peaceful revolution, sweeping away so many human rights abuses and the repressive style of Government that is not fitted to the 21st century.

In a very small way Muffin Heaven will try to support the oppressed both locally and internationally, because there must be more to this life than simply stuffing our faces with sweet things. It might be possible to add some lettering under our cafe sign so it reads: MUFFIN HEAVEN – more than just cake ! This would be preferable to 'let them eat cake'. I'm fairly sure my co-investor (Jonny) will not allow it, having already suggested: MUFFIN HEAVEN – since 1911. He reckons that if anyone questions when we opened the defence will be that it was eleven minutes past seven at night !

'Have you heard from Kazia recently ?'

'Don't be nosy.'

'She's my friend too !'

'She's my special friend.'

8.1

Like stars in the unpolluted Yorkshire Wolds sky, it is impossible for me to count how many times I've repeated the mantra: 'Positive, Modest, Self-belief' or similar upbeat words. I feel it's important to include modest, as this is a crucial counter-balance to excessive success – if it ever happens ! I have so far managed to avoid any significant episodes of depression, despite the fact I no longer have a secure job, the money has virtually run out and there is no certainty of Muffin Heaven being profitable.

Saturday night just gone provided a useful distraction from day to day problems with the pre-Christmas gathering of the clans. We are perhaps lucky in that any differences in our family are often unspoken, as opposed to the all out battles that are supposed to take place between some relatives at this emotional time.

Much drink was taken by those not having to drive, and the usual jolly and relaxed atmosphere developed – it can be much more relaxing with a family group because there's very little need to pretend as they've surely seen the worst and best of you over so many years.

There has been much in the news recently about a former high-flying TV newsreader now sleeping on a park bench because of the massive debts he ran up. He is still in touch with grown-up kids, yet has clearly become estranged from family and society to a dangerous degree. The fascination appears to have been how can a formerly well-off person find themselves on the streets ? This question taps into many of our fears and insecurities and is always of particular interest at this time of year when we are all supposed to gather in happy families, but very many don't.

If Muffin Heaven is not a success it's possible that I could find myself homeless – Heather is unlikely to give me a good reference for a return to office life, and there's bugger all in terms of work in our rural community. I must repeat my mantra once again, or reach for the neglected The Promised Land by Dr Rick Norris, who has surely encountered many folk who have lost everything.

The week before Christmas is beginning frosty and cold - I will be happy to take these weather conditions rather than the snow many are hoping for that will only turn to horrible slush and minor flooding. As expected I have not received a single card, and not sent any except to those within the family who are solely able to provide some degree of constancy in a world of uncertainty.

8.2

Because of Jonny One-Thumb's unscheduled return he was able to start work on one of our last major projects within Muffin Heaven – construction of a simple, fully functioning toilet area. This further burst of activity will keep his mind off his difficult brother and Kazia so far away in the frozen wastes of Poland.

Kunchen seemed pleased to have this return to manual labour and the two of them worked well together – Jonny doing the technical bits and Kunchen any heavy lifting or passing the right tool. I was the only person interrupting their progress, always keen to have a chat and yet another cup of tea while asking silly questions about plumbing.

'So we're going for just the one toilet ?'

'We agreed there wasn't room for separate facilities' Jonny confirmed.

'I'm a little worried about a chap peeing all over the place and a woman having to follow him in.'

'We'll have to check and clean at least once an hour.'

'Might be difficult at busy times.'

'I happy to clean' Kunchen said.

'Sorted' said Jonny.

'So long as we agree there must be constant monitoring.'

'Constant.'

'What about fresh flowers ?'

'Steady on, we're just providing a basic facility.'

'I'll have a word with Mary; just remember this bog might be the only one for ten miles.'

'Rubbish.'

Jonny and Kunchen were delighted when the conversation ended and they could get on with the task in hand; I took a walk outside, where the view was still splendid despite a thick canopy of grey cloud.

8.3

We have almost reached the winter solstice, which occurs just a few days before the commercial outpouring of Christmas, and will doubtless pass unnoticed by most of the population focused on matters that have nothing to do with the celebration of Christ's birth. It remains grey and cold – not good conditions for taking the Benelli Velvet 250 along deserted country lanes; I can certainly see the attraction of seeking winter sun – islands where it's possible to ride a bike at any time of year.

Many villagers have decorated the inside and outside of their houses with bright lights, which are quite a shock in a community that has no street lighting. We have a small conifer in the living room and flashing lights, but the trend seems to be making the outer walls of your abode as bold as possible, demonstrating to all your neighbours who can be the brightest and best.

We are leaving the Muffin Heaven sign lit throughout the dark months, but not bothering with more elaborate decoration – people seem to forget that simplicity can be a powerful tool.

'It's a shame Kazia can't be here.'

'She'll be back soon enough; you can understand why she wants to back with her family' Jonny replied.

'Very strong Catholic support in Poland.'

'So she tells me.'

'We'll have a full house anyway – there's all our lot, plus you and Kunchen.'

'Don't suppose he'll eat Turkey.'

'He'll have to have some extra sprouts – the kids won't want any.'

'Neither will I.'

'Some people are so fussy !'

'I'll be happy with a few glasses of wine.'

'And the rest.'

It would be some weeks before the cold days would noticeably lengthen, and then it would be time for the historic opening of a former barn as an unusual cafe-cum-community centre.

8.4

I was knackered after receiving two loads of logs from the Birdsall estate – one dumped at home and one up at Muffin Heaven. It took me an hour to stack a load in the garage, then thirty minutes outside the old barn with Kunchen helping. It's alright for these young lads capable of crossing high mountain ranges with few supplies, but I'm not getting any younger. There is however something satisfying in ending up with many neatly stacked logs, and a feeling of warm security for the next few months.

I usually go for my ride to nowhere on the exercise bike every morning, but this must now be postponed as too much physical activity could be dangerous as I get nearer and nearer to fifty.

'You're too fat' Jonny observed bluntly.

'I'm too tired to argue, but you're right anyway.'

'Perhaps you should fast over Christmas ?'

'Fuck off ! There's little enough pleasure in this life.'

'You've both done a good job with the wood - these log burners are wonderful, I could just watch the flames all day.'

'Get the bloody toilet finished you lazy sod !'

'We're well ahead of schedule for opening.'

'You never know, we could easily have the roof blown off in January.'

'I thought you were supposed to be having a more positive attitude ?'

'It helps to be aware of potential pitfalls.'

Kunchen was still busy carrying in baskets of logs to dry out, while we sat with yet another cup of tea.

'Come and sit down lad, have a break' said Jonny.

He smiled, sitting near us on the floor without saying a word, but it was never one of those uncomfortable silences you get with some unfriendly and disinterested folk.

8.5

I am hoping that the ushanka I have ordered on the Internet will keep me warm through the worst winter weather yet to come, and that the extra large size will fit my big head. Apparently, many English speakers usually call it a shapka, which is the Russian word for hat – this version comes with earflaps and a Soviet army badge ! I must have seen them in films like Dr Zhivago (did Julie Christie ever look better ?!) and have developed romantic associations about the grey version in particular. They are well known as headgear worn by Soviet soldiers, though their origins are said to be Mongolia in the Middle Ages.

Without such a hat I will not survive the many journeys to and from the dizzy heights of Muffin Heaven, as I am not one of those men blessed with hair on top. I know that for some chaps baldness can be devastating, but I'm not bothered apart from the vulnerability to freezing conditions. There were some real rabbit fur examples on offer, but I have gone for the synthetic imitation that is very similar from a distance in bad weather.

I find that my feet are often cold at the moment, but I'm reluctant to spend over one hundred pounds for the yak leather boots that have been advertised recently. The manufacturer claims they are three times stronger than ordinary leather and can stand-up to any adverse weather conditions. I'll have to mention the idea to Kunchen some time as he must be very much more familiar with yak products than myself.

I only recently discovered the hats were called ushanka, a fact that didn't emerge last time I bought similar headwear

– eventually proving a few centimetres too small. I'm sure Jonny or Kunchen will be happy to take the new one off my hands if it doesn't fit; another issue will be just how ridiculous it looks so far from Moscow or Ulan Bator.

I suppose it can be the emotional chill in our hearts that is sometimes more devastating than the savage winds of Siberia; of course there has been no word from beautiful Heather or attractive Kate – you certainly find out who your friends are when embarking upon a new career – in this case more quickly than expected.

There is some cheer in today's weather as the relentless grey skies have given way to patches of blue; and always the opportunity to throw another log on the fire when it looks like going out on an especially bitter afternoon. From the winter solstice it will be as if so many people are slowly adding fuel to an enormous bonfire that will eventually bring longer days of precious warmth and light.

8.6

This morning – a few days before the 'big day' – we are trapped under thick grey cloud again, and I can't even see Muffin Heaven from the village. Some villagers appear to have given up work already for the holidays, as there are several more cars than on a usual day of labour. I've just dropped the young lad at school early as all kids are travelling to Scarborough for some kind of Christmas play or pantomime.

'Do you think it's too late to get a flight to Poland ?'

'You're crazy Jonny, can't you be parted for a few weeks ?'

'I had a text from Kazia suggesting I meet the family.'

'Ring the travel agent if you want, but everything will be booked up.'

'I tried to tell her that.'

'It's not as if she's away for months.'

'Have you ever been in love ?'

'Don't get me started on that subject !'

'I've never been to Poland.'

'You've got something in common with 99 percent of the UK population then.'

'If you exclude all the Poles from your equation.'

'Do what you like, but expect to be disappointed.'

'Is that your philosophy of life ?'

'It used to be.'

Our moods seemed to reflect the grey, cold atmosphere outside; only the festive lights that many people left on all day offered some artificial consolation to those in need of Christmas cheer.

'I'll try ringing for a flight then.'

'Whatever.'

8.7

The jammy twat managed to get a flight booked from Leeds-Bradford via Schipol in Holland to Warsaw on the 23rd of December. The only force that might now intervene was of course the weather in three countries, which could easily turn nasty at this time of year. The power of true love had triumphed, and secretly I wished to be flying off somewhere to meet the love of my life.

I had to remind myself that there was much to be thankful for at home, particularly with the exciting prospect of a new business and finally discarding the appalling routine of office life. A modest snowfall in the next few weeks would make the Yorkshire Wolds no less magical than many winter destinations – loud with the joyful sounds of children sledging.

'Do you know much Polish then ?'

'English is understood virtually everywhere.'

'Not where Kazia's family live in that remote village.'

'A few drinks and nobody will care about language barriers.'

'Watch out for the dad, he's bound to be careful where his only daughter is concerned.'

'You're just trying to scare me – first you said there'd be no flights, now her family are violent.'

'That's not what I said; can't you take a joke ?'

'Just nervous I suppose.'

'Who wouldn't be with a convicted criminal as a potential father-in-law ?'

'What are you talking about.'

'Something Kazia mentioned; I'm sure it'll be fine.'

'Spit it out.'

'Apparently he stabbed some bloke, but it was an accident.'

'Great, it sounds just like my brother.'

'Don't worry, you'll have a lovely time.'

'Thanks very much.'

8.8

I have just received the novel Niels Lyhne by Danish author Jens Peter Jacobsen, which I'd read was recommended by the famous poet Rilke. As the front cover is a picture of Edvard Munch's Melancholy the likelihood is that it will not be a barrel of laughs. The summary on the back cover says that six strong-willed women caution the hero on the dangers of idealized love, which is extraordinary compared with my own unfortunate lessons in the subject.

My first major experience of this kind of love was while still at secondary school where I fell for an extremely attractive dark-haired lass who had a limited intellect, but fine breasts and bum. After a few years of unfulfilled misery I ended up in a mental hospital (now the designer outlet shopping centre) receiving strong drugs and electric shock treatment.

If only there had been tutorials at school or home that warned me of the terrible dangers - I would have been content with one strong-willed woman advising me, but sadly nobody has ever offered this kind of support. We covered so many dubiously important subjects, like Maths, English, German, Sport, Cooking, Needlework, Geography, History – but not the history of human emotion. I suppose you can learn it indirectly, through people you observe in the 'real world', in books, or more likely these days – television soaps.

My most recent painful episode has been with former colleague Heather who I have certainly idealized at times, and am now unlikely to see again. The trouble is that this worshipping is always to the detriment of one's own well-being, undermining crucial self-belief and positive attitude.

Yet a certain amount of this unrealistic approach must be inherent in any love that develops – you only have to look at Jonny and Kazia.

Because of the extreme outcome of my first love I am much stronger now, and though my feelings for Heather have been painful it seems I'm able to avoid the utter catastrophe of teenage years. So what else remains except growing disillusionment ? Like the main character of our Danish story who has rejected even the religious faith that might have sustained.

I have discovered the winter solstice takes place on December 22nd this year at around six in the morning UK time, which is now only fourteen hours away – fourteen hours until the growing darkness turns to a very slowly growing lightness. I must take comfort in this eternal story of the natural world, and the behaviour of plants and animals that are so much more in touch with true being.

To a greater or lesser degree I will always be falling in love with inappropriate women, always searching for the ideal match to my own flawed and dreamy personality – it's just that these days I've learned to manage the consequences – until the elusive true love is finally uncovered !

8.9

We were bullied into going to McDonald's yesterday by our young lad who simply couldn't exist without one of the crap toys that comes with a Happy Meal. I stuck to a coffee and blueberry muffin – which was stale, presumably because most people order burgers or fries – in fairness to the burger giant they do have a rigorous freshness policy, but with this blueberry muffin it had seriously broken down.

York city centre so close to Christmas Day was a nightmare of people buying things they don't really need, which is a shame when they could easily buy stuff that is needed – for themselves, or better still other folk who could really use a break. I stood outside a shoe shop: Office, while my daughter took nearly one hour to choose some simple-looking shoes; all the time I feared that ex-colleagues would approach unexpectedly, but once again I escaped unharmed.

We went to watch skaters on the ice rink that was lit by an almost full moon – a magical winter scene by any standards – reassuring our six year-old son that he could definitely have a go when slightly bigger. The moon must have triggered something in his developing brain, because later he insisted on watching American Werewolf in London on DVD – one of the best films ever made - combining horror, comedy, suspense, special effects, yet managing to maintain real emotional engagement.

Having purchased a cheap turkey all we need now is to get some extra coal to ensure comfortable days and nights in the chilly Yorkshire Wolds; there should be plenty of grub to go round as Jonny has succumbed to his burgeoning feelings of love – taking flight to icy Poland, hoping for a very warm welcome !

My ushanka has arrived and is everything that was promised on the website, but even this extra large model is not quite big enough for my massive head ! It will fit with a little bit of force and I hope that the tightness lessens over the years – despite being synthetic it feels so warm that I'll only be able to wear it in really extreme conditions and not for the daily school drop-off and collection. One day I will find the perfect hat – there must be one waiting for me somewhere in the world that will be an effortless fit and just feel right.

The Yorkshire Wolds is frosty this morning with bright blue sky; Christmas Day is unlikely to see any snow here, but a widespread frost will give the illusion of a miraculous world of white that so many romantic souls yearn for. Our kids are getting so excited over the many toys that they'll receive, and we adults can be content with a roaring fire accompanied by a port or brandy.

9

The most surprising occurrence over the Christmas period was receiving a letter from the mother of one of my daughter's 'friends', including print-outs from a social networking website showing that our daughter had been hideously abusive. We haven't yet contacted the family concerned, but have banned our daughter from doing just about everything – particularly any use of computer or Internet.

It's extraordinary how bitter these disputes can become between almost teenage girls, which happen because of the most trivial disagreements that seem so significant to their small minds. The Internet has provided many benefits, but these networking sites often allow the exchange of horrible comments and ideas. It seems ironic that our daughter has just won a gift token at school for her anti-bullying poem, and now she is carrying out so-called cyber-bullying that is so often reported in the media.

We have obviously failed as parents to apply enough discipline – most of the time allowing both our brats to do just about anything within the law. A good punishment might be to make them attend church services, as we were forced to do in the more innocent times of the 1960s. Mary received one overtly religious card this year: 'Jesus is the reason for the season !' it loudly proclaims on the front - I bet this family don't have any problems with naughty children.

This is the quiet period between Christmas and New Year when most people seem not to have returned to work and the stress of Christmas Day is thankfully over for another year. Weather in the Yorkshire Wolds is grey and extremely mild, which will only encourage premature blooms to appear in village gardens.

Kunchen has chosen to spend much of the time up at Muffin Heaven, guarding the building like a Tibetan Spaniel or Tibetan Terrier. He did join us for the big meal on Christmas Day, but only consumed a few vegetables and some water. For some reason the Queen's Speech on TV made him laugh out loud, then soon after he wandered up the deserted path towards the snug barn lit only by the wood burning stoves.

While we munched on the turkey it emerged that Kunchen comes from Lhatok in Tibet where Apo Gaga was also born – later to become the 17th Gyalwa Karmapa. They had played together often as young boys, which is why Kunchen has been able to secure his ribbon-cutting services for early February. He just laughs when talking about his former playmate – now such an important figure in Tibetan Buddhism – but to Kunchen he will always be a grubby, lively lad who was just like any other.

9.1

Jonny returned unexpectedly before New Year with Kazia, which was a boost to our planned small-scale celebrations, though something of a puzzle.

'I thought you weren't coming back for at least another week ?'

'Minor family disagreement' Jonny commented.

'No actual fighting I hope ?'

'Only verbally.'

They both looked happy enough, but seemed reluctant to divulge exactly what had happened.

'I'm sure they'll open up in their own time' Mary said.

'I'll attempt to force as much drink down Jonny's neck on New Year's Eve as possible.'

'Don't make him ill.'

We had decided to hold our small party at Muffin Heaven because there was much more room and it would give us a feel for the place as a social venue. Kunchen didn't seem too keen on the amount of alcohol that had been delivered to the old barn, particularly as there were so few people to consume vast quantities of beer, wines and spirits.

The weather had remained mild and grey in the Wolds, though there were some reports of minor snowfall in other parts of Yorkshire; any hopes of sledging on the first day of a new year had been well and truly dismissed by our local forecasters. All the kids seemed to be out in the village with new toys that had been recently acquired, including dangerous mini-motorbikes that are illegal on public roads.

'What's the weather doing in Poland then ?'

'Much snow' Kazia replied.

'We had a sleigh ride' Jonny chipped in.

The returned couple were very content in each other's company and much more touchy-feely than had been evident before the Christmas celebrations. Something dodgy had clearly occurred with Kazia's family, but it wasn't affecting them too much – they were looking forward to the imminent drinkathon as keenly as the rest of us.

9.2

On New Year's Eve we finally gave in to our barely suppressed desire to obtain a Tibetan Terrier puppy – the one remaining from a litter that had comprised two bitches and one dog. We drove down into the forgotten flatlands between Selby and Hull where the most stunning features are giant power stations and the brown Ouse ever widening towards the Humber estuary.

It is strange how a little dog can change a family forever in such a short time of playful destruction, peeing on the carpet, or sleeping like a tiny angel. He didn't enjoy the longish car ride back to the Wolds, but eventually went to sleep on the back seat with two large front paws projecting into space. If there is any trace memory of the Himalayas he will surely be more at home in our hilly location than Howden, Goole or Selby.

Kunchen was just as excited as our own kids, and clearly familiar with the ancient breed that has been a watchdog and companion in Tibet for centuries.

'We had dog like this.'

'At home ?'

'We play with him at monastery, with Apo Gaga......... Karmapa.'

'What colour was your dog ?'

'Not black like this – light colour.'

Kunchen seemed almost always happy, but I'd never seen him quite so full of fun as when he rolled on the rug with our new puppy – as if he was back in the mountainous homeland of a carefree early childhood.

'It's like having another kid' said Mary.

'He's gonna shred everything we've got.'

The hours before midnight on New Year's Eve were quite different from those that had been planned, as all attention was on the little dog rather than all the booze lined-up at Muffin Heaven. At least there was plenty of room for him to rampage around the old barn before eventually flopping down in a small heap of tousled black fur. We didn't know if it was before midnight or after midnight, if it was the old year or the new; plenty of alcohol was consumed, but the atmosphere was one of gentle fun rather than the wild music and dancing we'd hoped for.

9.3

The first week of the new year turned bright and cold with promises of snow, which to residents of Moscow might be a daily occurrence, but to us an occasional miraculous transformation. I was interested to see how Kunchen and the new puppy would react to a frozen landscape of white – my fairly safe prediction was with loud joy and enthusiasm.

As I'm no longer an office worker there has not been the painful return to the daily grind that many will suffer, just plenty of last minute details to sort out before our cafe opens in just a few weeks.

'I'll go and do a few jobs at the barn' said Jonny.

'Can I help ?' Kazia asked enthusiastically.

'I've got Kunchen, perhaps you could try out a few new recipes – start putting the menu together properly.'

'I hope there's no snow for our grand opening' I worried.

'Not much we can do about it' Jonny replied.

'Do you think this Karmapa will actually turn up ?'

'Kunchen certainly does, and I have no reason to doubt him.'

'He's proved to be a fine young man.'

'More so than us !' laughed Jonny.

The only hold-ups we were experiencing were because of the extremely demanding dog that had just landed in our lives – not that there were any really major works to complete at Muffin Heaven. He wasn't very happy being locked in the kitchen at night, but we didn't have much choice due to our vicious cat, and a need to preserve some carpets and furniture in the house. Once our business was up and running the little pup would be an ideal distraction for customers as they waited for tea, coffee, muffins or whatever Polish delights Kazia had come up with.

'Bertie is not a very Tibetan name for the dog' Jonny said. 'That's kids for you.'

9.4

A decent snowfall has changed our village overnight into a paradise for children, though not so good for anyone who has to get in or out of the Yorkshire Wolds. I've already been sledging with the young lad, which was great apart from trudging back up the hill every time, and surprisingly we didn't even fall off.

We're not even bothering to trek towards Muffin Heaven today – Kunchen will be fine up there with the wood burners going and no shortage of supplies. For once he can just relax and imagine himself back in the mighty Himalayas, perhaps growing a little sad because of the enforced separation from his homeland.

Our young lad has been back to the house looking for a carrot and five pieces of coal to help complete the snowman he's building with a friend; then he's back again five minutes later asking to go on the slopes with another family. Our pup Bertie has been out a couple of times in the garden, utilising his enormous snow-shoe paws to scamper in the snow; proper walks will have to wait for a few weeks – when the vet's injections have kicked-in properly.

'We're getting married in the spring' Jonny announced.

'Great news !'

'The only problem is it has to be in Poland.'

'I'm sure we can manage for a few weeks.'

'It's not that. I'm worried about family arguments again.'

'What exactly happened over Christmas ?'

'The older brother seems to think she should be with a genuine Polish boy.'

'I was expecting the father to be the problem - they'll all come round.'

'Eventually, but it does tend to spoil things now.'

Mary bravely set off for York before the gritter lorry had been through the village; many others would not return to work or school for another few days. The problem might be getting home after dark, particularly if the back roads turn icy under a thin covering of snow. For us lucky ones, at home with a real fire, able to look out at a magical winter scene of so much virgin white, except for the busy kids rolling larger and larger balls of snow into scary snowballs or fat, friendly figures of ice.

9.5

It's hard to believe that most snow has disappeared overnight leaving the usual soggy aftermath we experience in England – except on the high moors and fells where it can stubbornly remain for many weeks. I can see a rather sad snowman melting outside a little girl's house, that she earlier inspected with disbelief at the rapid disintegration of her beloved creation.

It continues to prove difficult to achieve anything with the lively presence of our new puppy that is either biting the kids or squaring up with a hissing cat. Whenever I'm awake at night he's either barking, scratching the door of the kitchen or whining – I think the seller misled us slightly as to Bertie's placid temperament – all being well he'll settle down with age !

I have performed a New Year consultation of the I Ching, which indicates that there will be unexpected good fortune; I don't know whether this means success with Muffin Heaven or something truly unexpected. I will continue to repeat my positive mantra in the hope of personal and worldwide prosperity, but there are so many bastards to contend with.

'The idea of a big Catholic wedding is rather daunting' said Jonny.

'Even former Prime Minister Blair has converted to the faith.'

'He'll be trying to take over as Pope.'

'I'm not sure if that's possible, but it always seems more style than substance with him.'

'At least there should be a good piss-up afterwards – the Poles seem to really like a drink.'

'That's when the scrapping will start !'

'Not funny.'

'Don't worry too much, Kazia will support you.'

'And me her.'

'Sounds like true love.'

Jonny smiled.

'I'd better go and see what Kunchen is doing up there on his own.'

'You don't fancy taking this bloody dog with you ?'

'Your problem' laughed Jonny.

'More Tibetan Terror than Tibetan Terrier.'

Jonny was lucky to always have DIY tasks to escape into, while I was left to literally clean up the shit.

9.6

At last our village is looking more deserted in the morning, which means that the festive period is officially over and many people have returned to work. It will be a relief to some, as there is almost a requirement to be cheerful over the special fortnight of coming together with our nearest and dearest.

It is frightening to think that we have a cafe to open at the beginning of February, and also the hope that it will be much more than a mere cafe. I read recently that the Yorkshire Wolds is one of the least visited areas of England, which is perhaps not the best foundation for a successful 'visitor attraction'.

The Christmas holiday has eaten up any remaining cash, and it is not right to keep asking Jonny One-Thumb for more – so we have an urgent need to sell plenty of muffins. In the next few weeks I must contact all the local newspapers, radio and TV, explaining why we have the 17th incarnation of the Gyalwa Karmapa opening our little venue.

At least our Tibetan Terrier is finally settling down – not making so much noise at night – unlike myself, snoring appallingly according to various family members. The kids are going back to school tomorrow though, which means I'll have to play and clean up after Bertie all day.

Another complication is that Mary is expecting to travel (for work) to Sicily at the end of January or beginning of February – if you can call that work. We could really have used her help at our critical time, but unless Kazia and Jonny decide to get married early all should be well.

The weather is currently grey and mild, but I suppose there is a fair chance of more snow when Muffin Heaven finally opens its doors. I might ring North Yorkshire County Council to see if they can do an extra gritting of the roads (if needed) to ensure all invited guests can negotiate the tricky inclines around here.

In the distance I can hear military planes performing their regular manoeuvres, but today it seems our village will miss out on the terrifying low-flying exercises that frequently scare children, animals and sensitive adults. Because the UK wastes billions of pounds on 'defence' these sorties are deemed 'essential', yet there are still millions of people in this country struggling to obtain the essentials of life, and far more needy people in other parts of the world. Our little pup has not heard one of these jets over our house yet, but he will not have to wait long for the nonsense of war games.

My highlight of the holiday period has been watching repeats of the unlikely TV detective Hetty Wainthropp, which is based somewhere near Burnley in East Lancashire. You can keep all your American cop shows set in LA, Miami or New York – just to hear the sound of brass band music rising above the redundant mills stirs the heart of any true northerner.

9.7

We were contacted by the Tibetan Government in Exile website based in London for an interview/explanation of why one of their highest ranking religious figures was opening a Yorkshire Wolds venue called Muffin Heaven. They were somewhat reassured to hear the connection between Kunchen and Karmapa, and also my assurance that the opening would be a very low-key affair.

I still remained doubtful that this major figure of Tibetan Buddhism would turn up, but Jonny's belief in Kunchen was rock solid because of their close working relationship over recent times. Jonny's main focus was of course Kazia, and they rarely seemed to be apart as she got used to the kitchen equipment at Muffin Heaven and he went through a long snagging list of DIY tasks.

When I wasn't drumming-up publicity it was possible for me to sit back and gaze out of the enormous west window over the soggy January fields towards York; we were promised a very unsettled week of heavy rain, which had its own drama and fascination when viewed from a warm, weather-tight barn.

'Any more news on the wedding Kazia ?'

'I think we should concentrate on getting this place open' Jonny interrupted.

'My family will be OK, they can see we are well suited' she said.

'They'll have to accept I'm not becoming a Catholic.'

'But we still get married in the church' said Kazia.

'Jonny has no problem with that' I said, in an attempt to offer some support.

Kazia went quiet for a while, mixing together some ingredients for an apple and lemon muffin.

'I can smell the lemon really strongly, even before they go in the oven.'

'Good recipe' responded Kazia.

'I've just got to pop into York for some screws' said Jonny.

There seemed to be a few problems to sort out before all were happy with the planned wedding, though I was sure that they were so committed to each other that even family or religion could not prevent a happy union.

9.8

We managed to get a half-price Gaggia coffee machine in the post-Christmas sales, which will at least give the illusion of a professional cafe, though it will be Kazia rather than myself who'll figure out how the bloody thing works.

'I can't see us getting many customers until the late spring or summer' said Jonny.

'We're certainly going to make most of our money during the summer months, but we'll have to promote special events at other times – and don't forget the 'educational' classes !'

'I do hope the opening goes well.'

'If this Karmapa doesn't turn-up we're stuffed.'

'At least there aren't any other cafes for several miles.'

'Not much of anything for miles !'

The Wolds could feel particularly lonely in the winter months because of the lack of daylight and folk not inclined to venture out, but this was already improving in the afternoon, whereas each morning still struggled to remove its blanket of darkness. Each day when we went up to Muffin Heaven Kunchen's beaming face was waiting behind the heavy wooden door – sometimes the only natural glow on a bitter winter day.

There was almost snow in the garden this morning, but it was more like a crust of frozen ice that had formed after the storm late last night; it's hard to believe that we are less than twenty miles from York, such can be the difference in weather between the dead flat Vale and our own hills of chalk.

'We'll have to order another load of logs' Jonny said.

'If we get any spare cash remind me to buy a forest.'

'It's well worth paying for the timber – this damp barn has

been transformed by the stoves.'

'I can't argue with that.'

'The only disadvantage is that a woman's nipples don't stick out so much in a warm space.'

'You keep your sick mind on the wedding – forget about the chapel hat pegs.'

9.9

'Soup !' announced Jonny loudly.
'But we've just had breakfast.'
'No – that's what people will want at this time of year.'
'Some will.'
'A different homemade soup every day.'
'It'll be a lot of work for somebody.'
'Kazia won't mind.'
'Not everyone will like Polish cuisine.'
'Don't forget she worked on York market.'
'Where they serve chip butties and bacon sarnies.'
'Do you think we should do chip butties ?'
'If the demand is there.'
'And we can get rid of fatty smells.'
'Let's not lose sight of muffins and coffee, that's our main brand if you like.'
'Fine, but we need to offer some winter warmers.'
'Folks will come just to sit by the wood burners and look out of the window.'
Muffin Heaven was already something unique in a sparsely populated area, but the likelihood of survival in the early years would probably depend upon the payment of low wages – if any. Kunchen's dream of an early return to his homeland was just one of the plans that would have to be put on hold, unless the miracle of many visitors occurred.
Positive thinking is still something to value, but no substitute for positive things actually happening; not even a brief message from Heather or other former colleagues has arrived, which inevitably has a mildly depressing effect – the

realisation that they don't particularly worship you, and any worshipping of them is misplaced. Time to forget the past and embrace a new way of life !

10

Our grand opening didn't exactly go according to plan, though the day started well with a spectacular blue sky. The Karmapa didn't turn-up, which was no fault of Kunchen's, but it did take away our star guest and hopes of massive publicity. TV, radio and newspapers did come, and it seemed all was going to fall horribly flat until Kunchen picked up a fresh blueberry muffin and bit into it.

Suddenly all the cameras started flashing and all attention was turned towards our quiet Tibetan companion; Jonny started to explain how Kunchen had escaped Tibet and the whole place fell silent and listened attentively to the dramatic tale of his flight to freedom.

Kazia was busily going round all the visitors dishing out muffins and drinks; there were plenty of people from the village and a few local councillors. The atmosphere became more relaxed as some commented on the splendid view over the Vale of York and others asked about the pretty young Polish woman dashing about.

Modest Kunchen had managed to provide a story for the media, while his illustrious childhood friend was stuck in London because of a train crash near Peterborough. It was particularly pleasing that the local TV station Look North promised to show a short feature on our event on the Monday evening programme.

We were all knackered but quietly satisfied as the day slipped into frosty darkness and the last guests disappeared back to the safety of towns.

'It all went surprisingly well' said Jonny.

'We have given out more than two hundred muffins !' Kazia announced.

'Well done everybody; it all looked rather bleak at the start. You leave me to clear up and go back to house for a celebration.'

It felt strange to be left alone in Muffin Heaven after all the excitement of the day, and for a while I just sat with a beer looking towards the orange and white lights of York. I heard the big wooden door open, turning in expectation of Kunchen returning, but it wasn't him.

'Bloody hell !'

'Hello.'

'Heather........I didn't expect....'

'It's really warm in here, can I take off my coat ?'

'Of course.'

She removed a thick winter parka, leaving only a fine white dress that left nothing to the imagination.

'So this is Muffin Heaven ?'

'It is now.'

Printed in the United States
103168LV00001B/31/P

9 781897 312650